AF293141

tredition®

tredition was established in 2006 by Sandra Latusseck and Soenke Schulz. Based in Hamburg, Germany, tredition offers publishing solutions to authors and publishing houses, combined with worldwide distribution of printed and digital book content. tredition is uniquely positioned to enable authors and publishing houses to create books on their own terms and without conventional manufacturing risks.

For more information please visit: www.tredition.com

TREDITION CLASSICS

This book is part of the TREDITION CLASSICS series. The creators of this series are united by passion for literature and driven by the intention of making all public domain books available in printed format again - worldwide. Most TREDITION CLASSICS titles have been out of print and off the bookstore shelves for decades. At tredition we believe that a great book never goes out of style and that its value is eternal. Several mostly non-profit literature projects provide content to tredition. To support their good work, tredition donates a portion of the proceeds from each sold copy. As a reader of a TREDITION CLASSICS book, you support our mission to save many of the amazing works of world literature from oblivion. See all available books at www.tredition.com.

 Project Gutenberg

The content for this book has been graciously provided by Project Gutenberg. Project Gutenberg is a non-profit organization founded by Michael Hart in 1971 at the University of Illinois. The mission of Project Gutenberg is simple: To encourage the creation and distribution of eBooks. Project Gutenberg is the first and largest collection of public domain eBooks.

The Flying Mercury

Eleanor M. (Eleanor Marie) Ingram

Imprint

This book is part of TREDITION CLASSICS

Author: Eleanor M. (Eleanor Marie) Ingram
Cover design: Buchgut, Berlin – Germany

Publisher: tredition GmbH, Hamburg - Germany
ISBN: 978-3-8472-1443-4

www.tredition.com
www.tredition.de

THE FLYING MERCURY

THE FLYING MERCURY

THE FLYING MERCURY

By

ELEANOR M INGRAM

Author of

THE GAME AND THE CANDLE

With Illustrations by

EDMUND FREDERICK

Decorations by

BERTHA STUART

INDIANAPOLIS
THE BOBBS-MERRILL COMPANY
PUBLISHERS

THE
FLYING
MERCURY

By

ELEANOR M INGRAM

Author of

THE GAME AND THE CANDLE

With Illustrations by

EDMUND FREDERICK

Decorations by

BERTHA STUART

INDIANAPOLIS

THE BOBBS-MERRILL COMPANY

PUBLISHERS

Copyright 1910

The Bobbs-Merrill Company

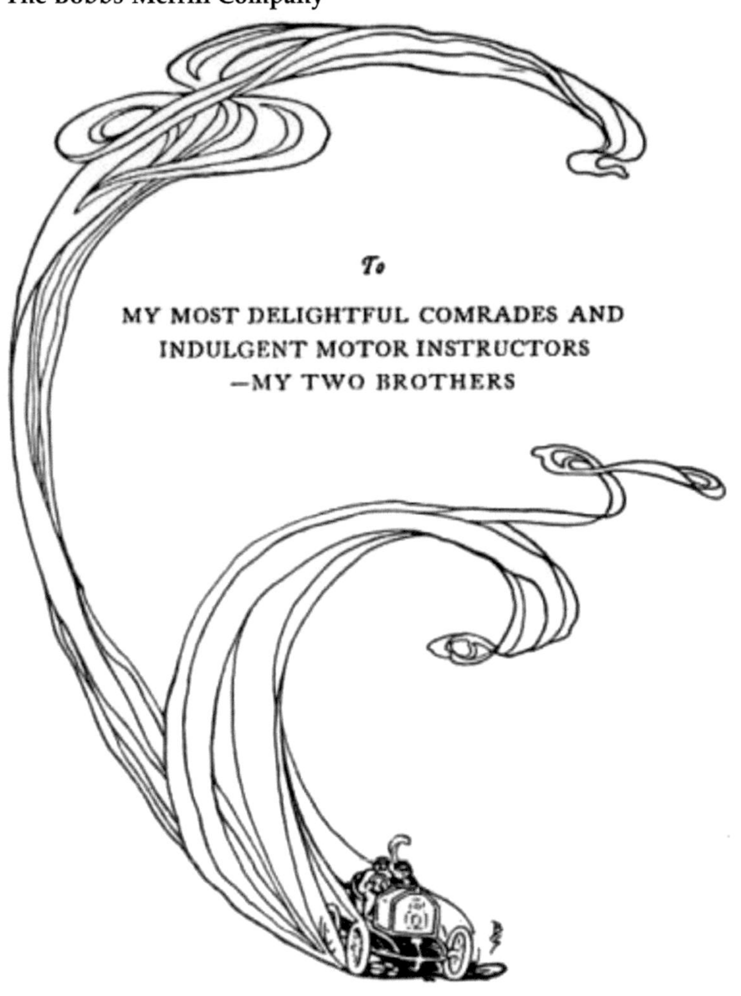

To

MY MOST DELIGHTFUL COMRADES AND
INDULGENT MOTOR INSTRUCTORS
—MY TWO BROTHERS

[1]

I

he roaring reports of the motor fell into abrupt silence, as the driver brought his car to a halt.

"You signaled?" he called across the grind of set brakes.

In the blending glare of the searchlights from the two machines, the gray one arriving and the limousine drawn to the roadside, the young girl stood, her hand still extended in the gesture which had stopped the man who now leaned across his wheel.

"Oh, please," she appealed again.

On either side stretched away the Long Island meadows, dark, soundless, appar [2] ently uninhabited. Only this spot of light broke the monotony of dreariness. A keen, chill, October wind sighed past, stirring the girl's delicate gown as its folds lay unheeded in the dust, fluttering her fur-lined cloak and shaking two or three childish curls from the bondage of her velvet hood. The driver swung himself down and came toward her with the unhasting swiftness of one trained to the unexpected.

"I beg pardon — can I be of some use?" he asked.

"We are lost," she confessed hurriedly. "If you could set us right, I should be grateful. I — we must get home soon. I have been a guest at a house somewhere here, and started to return to New York this afternoon. The chauffeur does not know Long Island; we can not seem to [3] find any place. And now we have lost a tire. I was afraid — "

She broke off abruptly, as her companion descended from the limousine.

"We only want to know the way; we're all right," he explained. "This is my cousin; I came out after her, you see. Don't get so worried, Emily — we'll go straight on as soon as Anderson changes the tire."

He huddled his words slightly and spoke too rapidly, the round, good-humored face he turned to the white light was too flushed; otherwise there was nothing unusual in his appearance. And his caste was evident and unquestionable, in spite of any circumstance. There was no anger in the girl's dark eyes as she gazed straight before her, only pity and helpless distress. [4]

"I can tell your chauffeur the road," the driver of the gray car quietly said. "Have you far to go?"

"To the St. Royal," she answered, looking at him. "My uncle is there. Is that far?"

"No; you can reach there by ten o'clock. I will speak to your chauffeur."

"Do, like a good fellow," the other man interposed. "Awfully obliged. You're not angry, Emily," he added, lowering his voice, and moving nearer her. "Since we're engaged, why should you get frightened simply because I proposed we get married to-night instead of waiting for a big wedding? I thought it was a good idea, you know. It isn't my fault Anderson got lost instead of getting us home for dinner, is it?"

"Hush, Dick," she rebuked, hot color [5] sweeping her face. "You, you are not well. And we are not engaged; you forget. Just because people want us to be—" Too proud to let her steadiness quiver, she broke the sentence.

If the driver had heard, and it was scarcely possible that he had not, he made no sign. By the acetylene light he produced an envelope and pencil, and proceeded to sketch a map, showing the route to the limousine's chauffeur.

"Understand it?" he queried, concluding. He had a certain decision of manner, not in the least arrogant, but the result of a serene self-surety that somehow accorded with his lithe, trained grace of movement. A judge of men would have read him an athlete, perhaps in an unusual line.

"Yes, sir," the chauffeur replied. "I'll [6] get Miss Ffrench home in no time after I get the tire on."

The indiscretion of the spoken name was ignored, except for a slight lift of the hearer's eyebrows.

"How long does it take you to change a tire?"

"About half an hour; it's night, of course."

An odd, choking gurgle sounded from the gray machine, where a dark figure had sat until now in quiescent muteness.

"Half an hour!" echoed the gray machine's driver, and faced toward the chuckle. "Rupert, it isn't in your contract, but do you want to come over and change this tire?"

"I'll do it for you, Darling," was the sweet response; the small figure rolled over the edge of the car with a cat-like [7] celerity. "Where are your tools, you chauffeur? Quick!"

The bewildered chauffeur mechanically reached for a box on the running-board, as the young assistant came up, grinning all over his malign dark face.

"Oh, quicker! What's the matter, rheumatism? They wouldn't have you in a training camp for motor trucks on Sunday. Hustle, *please*."

There never had been anything done to that sedate limousine quite as this was done. Even the preoccupied girl looked on in fascination at a rapidity of unwasted movement suggesting a conjuring feat.

"By George!" exclaimed her escort. "A splendid man you've got there! Really, a splendid chauffeur, you know."

The driver smiled with a gleam of irony, but disregarded the comment. [8]

"Would you like to get into your car?" he asked the girl. "You will be able to start very soon."

"I see that," she acknowledged gratefully. "Thank you; I would rather wait here."

"Is your chauffeur trustworthy?"

"Oh, yes; he has been in my uncle's employ for three years. But he was never before out here, in this place."

There was a pause, filled by the soft monotone of insults drifting from the side of the limousine, for Rupert talked while he worked and his fellow-worker did not please him.

"Wrench, baby hippo! Oh, look behind you where you put it— you need a memory course. You ought to be passing spools to a lady with a sewing-machine. Did you ever see a motor-car be [9] fore? There, pump her up, do." He rose, drew out his watch and glanced at it. "Five minutes; I'll have to beat that day after to-morrow."

The driver looked over at him and their eyes laughed together. Now, for the first time, the girl noticed that across the shoulders of both men's jerseys ran in silver letters the name of a famous foreign automobile.

"I am very grateful, indeed," she said bravely and graciously. "I wish I could say more, or say it better. The journey will be short, now."

But all her dignity could not check the frightened shrinking of her glance, first toward the interior of the limousine and then toward the man who was to enter there with her. And the driver of the gray machine saw it. [10]

"We have done very little," he returned. "May I put you in your car?"

The chauffeur was gathering his tools, speechlessly outraged, and making ready to start. Seated among the rugs and cushions, under the light of the luxurious car, the girl deliberately drew off her glove and held out her small uncovered hand to the driver of the gray machine.

"Thank you," she said again, meeting his eyes with her own, whose darkness contrasted oddly with the blonde curls clustered under her hood.

"You are not afraid to drive into the city alone?" he asked.

"Alone! Why, my cousin—"

"Your cousin is going to stay with me."

She flung back her head; amazement, question, relief struggled over her sensi [11] tive face, and finally melted into irrepressible mirth under the fine amusement of his regard.

"You are clever—and kind, to do that! No, I am not afraid."

He closed the door.

"Take your mistress home," he bade the chauffeur. "Crank for him, Rupert."

"Why, why—" stammered the limousine's other passenger, turning as the motor started.

No one heeded him.

"By-by, don't break any records," Rupert called after the chauffeur. "Hold yourself in, do. If you shed any more tires, telegraph for me, and if I'm within a day's run I'll come put them on for you and save you time."

Silence closed in again, as the red tail-light vanished around a bend. The gray [12] car's driver nodded curtly to the stupefied youth in the middle of the road.

"Unless you want to stay here all night, you'd better get in the machine," he suggested. "My name's Lestrange—I suppose yours is Ffrench?"

"Dick Ffrench. But, see here, you mean well, but I'm going with my cousin. I'd like a drive with you, but I'm busy."

"You're not fit to go with your cousin."

"Not—"

"Fit," completed Lestrange definitely. "Can you hang on somewhere, Rupert?"

"I can," Rupert assured, with an inflection of his own. "Get your friend aboard."

Lestrange was already in his seat, waiting.

"What's that for?" asked the dazed guest, as, on taking his place, a strap was [13] slipped around his waist, securing him to the seat.

"So you won't fall out," soothed the grinning Rupert. "You ain't well, you know. Not that I'd care if you did, but somebody might blame Darling."

The car leaped forward, gathering speed to an extent that was a revelation in motoring to Ffrench. The keen air, the giddy rush through the dark, were a sobering tonic. After a while he spoke to the man beside him, nervously embarrassed by a situation he was beginning to appreciate.

"This is a racing car?"

"It was."

"Isn't it now?"

"If I were going to race it day after to-morrow, I wouldn't be risking it over a country road to-night. A racing machine [14] is petted like a race-horse until it is wanted."

"And then?"

"It takes its chances. If you are connected with the Ffrenches who manufacture the Mercury car, you should know something of automobile racing yourself. I noticed your limousine was of that make."

"Yes, that is my uncle's company. I did see a race once at Coney Island. A car turned over and killed its driver and made a nasty muss. I—I didn't fancy it."

A wheel slipped off a stone, giving the car a swerving lurch which was as instantly corrected—with a second lurch—by its pilot. The effect was not tranquilizing; the shock swept the last confusion from Ffrench's brain. [15]

"Where are you taking me?" he presently asked.

"Where do you want to go? I will set you down at the next village we come to; you can stay there to-night or you can get a trolley to the city."

The question remained unanswered. Several times Ffrench glanced, rather diffidently, at his companion's clear, firm profile, and looked away again without speaking.

"I went out to get my cousin to-day, and my host gave me a couple of highballs," he volunteered, at last. "I don't know what you thought—"

Lestrange twisted his car around a belated farm-wagon.

"How old are you?" he inquired calmly.

"Twenty-three." [16]

"I'm nearly twenty-seven. That's what I thought."

The simpler mind considered this for a space.

"Some men are born awake, some awake themselves, and some are shaken into awakening," paraphrased Lestrange, in addition. "If I were you, I'd wake up; it comes easier and it's sure to arrive anyhow. There is the village ahead—shall I stop?"

"It looks terribly dull," was the doleful verdict.

"Then come with me," flashed the other unexpectedly; for a fractional instant his eyes left the road and turned to his companion's face. "Did you ever see race practice at dawn? Come try a night in a training camp."

"You'd bother with me?" [17]

"Yes."

A head bobbed up by Ffrench's knee, where Rupert was clinging in some inexplicable fashion.

"Once I rode eight miles out there by the hood, head downward, holding in a pin," he imparted, by way of entertainment.

Ffrench stared at the reeling perch indicated, and gasped.

"What for?" he asked.

"So we could keep on to our control instead of being put out of the running, of course. Did you guess I was curing a headache?"

"But you might have been killed!" exclaimed Ffrench.

Even by the semi-light of the lamps there was visible the mechanician's droll twist of lip and brow. [18]

"I'd drive to hell with Lestrange," he explained sweetly, and settled back in his place.

Ffrench drew a long breath. After a moment he again looked at the driver.

"I'll come," he accepted. "And, thank you."

It was Lestrange who smiled this time, with a sudden and enchanting warmth of mirth.

"We'll try to amuse you," he promised.

[19]

II

It was a business consultation that was being held in Mr. Ffrench's firelit library, in spite of the presence of a tea-table and the young girl behind it. A consultation between the two partners who composed the Mercury Automobile Company, of whom the lesser was speaking with a certain anecdotal weight.

"And he said he was losing too much time on the turns; so the next round he took the bend at seventy-two miles an hour. He went over, of course. The third car we've lost this year; I'm glad the season's closed."

Emily Ffrench gave an exclamation, her velvet eyes widening behind their black lashes. [20]

"But the driver! Was the poor driver hurt, Mr. Bailey?"

"He wasn't killed, Miss Emily," answered Bailey, with a tinge of pensive regret. He was a large, ruddy, white-haired man, with the slow and careful habit of speech sometimes found in those who live much with massive machinery. "No, he wasn't killed; he's in the hospital. But he wrecked as good a car as ever was built, through sheer foolishness. It costs money."

Mr. Ffrench responded to the indirect appeal with more than usual irritation, his level gray eyebrows contracting.

"We ought to have better drivers. Why do you not get better men, Bailey? You wanted to go into this racing business; you said the cars needed advertising. My brother always attended to that [21] side of the factory affairs, while he lived, with you as his manager. Now it is altogether in your hands. Why do you not find a proper driver?"

"Perhaps my hands are not used to holding so much," mused Bailey unresentfully. "A man might be a good manager, maybe, and weak as a partner. It isn't the same job. But a first-class driver isn't easy to get, Mr. Ffrench. There's Delmar killed, and George tied up with another company, and Dorian retired, all this last season; and we don't want a foreigner. There's only one man I like—"

"Well, get him. Pay him enough."

Bailey hunched himself together and crossed his legs.

"Yes, sir. He's beaten our cars—and others—every race lately, with poorer machines, just by sheer pretty driving. He [22] drives fast, yet he don't knock out his car. But there's a lot after him—there's just one way we could get him, and get him for keeps."

"And that?"

"He's ambitious; he wants to get into something more solid than racing. If we offered to make him manager, he'd come and put some new ideas, maybe, into the factory, and race our cars wherever we chose to enter them. I know him pretty well."

The proposition was advanced tentatively, with the hesitation of one venturing in unknown places. But Ethan Ffrench said nothing, his gray eyes fixed on the hearth.

"He understands motor construction and designing, and he's been with big foreign firms," Bailey resumed, after wait [23] ing. "He'd be useful around; I can't be everywhere. What he'd do for us in racing would help a whole lot. It's very well to make a fine standard car, but it needs advertising to keep people remembering. And men like to say 'my machine is the same as Lestrange won the Cup race with.' They like it."

"I don't know," said Mr. Ffrench slowly, "that it is dignified for the manager of the Mercury factory to be a racing driver."

"The Christine cars are driven by the son of the man who makes them," was the response. "Some drive their own."

"The son of the man who makes them," repeated the other. He turned his face still more to the quivering fire, his always severe expression hardening strangely and bitterly. "The son—" [24]

The girl rose to draw the crimson curtains before the windows and to push an electric switch, filling the room with a subdued golden glow in place of the late afternoon grayness. Her delicate face, as she regarded her uncle, revealed most strongly its characteristic over-earnestness and a sensitive reflection of the moods of those around her. Emily Ffrench's childhood had been passed in a Canadian convent, and something of its mysticism clung about her. As the cheerful change she had wrought flashed over the room, Mr. Ffrench held out his hand in a gesture of summons, so that she came across to sit on the broad arm of his chair during the rest of the conference, her soft gaze resting on the third member.

"My adopted son and nephew having no such talents, we must do the best we [25] can," Mr. Ffrench stated, with his most precise coldness. "Being well-born and well-bred, he has no taste for a mechanic's labor or for circus performances with automobiles in public. Who is your man, Bailey?"

"Lestrange, sir. You must have heard of him often."

"I never read racing news."

"I read ours," said Bailey darkly. "We've been licked often enough by him. And he's straight—he's one of the few men who'll stop at the grand-stand and lose time reporting a smash-up and sending help around. Every man on the track likes Darling Lestrange."

"Likes *whom*?"

Bailey flushed brick-red.

"I didn't mean to call him that. He signs himself D. Lestrange, and some of [26] them started reading it Darling, joking because he was such a favorite and because they liked him anyhow. It's just a nick-name."

Emily laughed out involuntarily, surprised.

"I beg pardon," she at once apologized, "but it sounded so frivolous."

"If you try this man, you had better keep that nickname out of the factory," Mr. Ffrench advised stiffly. "What respect could the workmen feel for a manager with such a title? If possible, you would do well to prevent them from recognizing him as the racing driver."

Bailey, who had risen at the chime of a clock, halted amazed.

"Respect for him!" he echoed. "Not recognize him! Why, there is-n't a man on the place who wouldn't give his ears [27] to be seen on the same side of the street with Lestrange, let alone to work under him. They *do* read the racing news. That part of it will be all right, if I can have him."

"If it is necessary —"

"I think it is, sir."

Emily moved slightly, pushing back her yellow-brown curls under the ribbon that banded them. On a sudden impulse her uncle looked up at her.

"What is your opinion?" he questioned. "If Dick had been listening I should have asked his, and I fancy yours is fully as valuable. Come, shall we have this racing manager?"

Astonished, she looked from her uncle to the other man. And perhaps it was the real anxiety and suspense of Bailey's expression that drew her quick reply. [28]

"Let us, uncle. Since we need him, let us have him."

"Very well," said Mr. Ffrench. "You hear, Bailey."

There was a long silence after the junior partner's withdrawal.

"Come where I can see you, Emily," her uncle finally demanded. "I liked your decided answer a few moments ago; you can reason. How long have you been a daughter in my house?"

"Six years," she responded, obediently moving to a low chair opposite. "I was fifteen when you took me from the convent — to make me very, very happy, dear."

"I sent for you when I sent for Dick, and for the same reason. I have tried three times to rear one of my name to fitness to bear it, and each one has failed [29] except you. I wish you were a man, Emily; there is work for a Ffrench to do."

"When you say that, I wish I were. But — I'm not, I'm not." She flung out her slender, round arms in a gesture of helpless resignation. "I'm not even a strong-minded woman who might do instead. Uncle Ethan, may I ask — it was Mr. Bailey who made me think — my cousin whom I never saw, will he never come home?"

Her voice faltered on the last words, frightened at her own daring. But her uncle answered evenly, if coldly:

"Never."

"He offended you so?"

"His whole life was an offense. School, college, at home, in each he went wrong. At twenty-one he left me and married a [30] woman from the vaudeville stage. It is not of him you are to think, Emily, but of a substitute for him. For that I designed Dick; once I hoped you would marry him and sober his idleness."

"Please, no," she refused gently. "I am fond of Dick, but—please, no."

"I am not asking it of you. He is well enough, a good boy, not overwise, but not what is needed here. Failed, again; I am not fortunate. There is left only you."

"Me?"

Her startled dark eyes and his determined gray ones met, and so remained.

"You, and your husband. Are you going to marry a man who can take my place in this business, in the factory and the model village my brother and I built around it; a man whose name will be fit to join with ours and so in a fashion pre [31] serve it here? Will you wait until such a one is found and will you aid me to find him? Or will you too follow selfish, idle fancies of your own?"

"No!" she answered, quite pale. "I would not do that! I will try to help."

"You will take up the work the men of your name refuse, you will provide a substitute for them?"

Her earnestness sprang to meet his strength of will, she leaned nearer in her enthusiasm of self-abnegation, scarcely understood.

"I will find a substitute or accept yours. I, indeed I will try not to fail."

It was characteristic that he offered neither praise nor caress.

"You have relieved my mind," said Ethan Ffrench, and turned his face once more to the fire.

[32]

III

It was October when the consultation was held in the library of the old Ffrench house on the Hudson; December was very near on the sunny morning that Emily drove out to the factory and sought Bailey in his office.

"I wanted to talk with you," she explained, as that gentleman rose to receive her. "We have known each other for a long time, Mr. Bailey; ever since I came from the Sacred Heart to live with Uncle Ethan. That is a *very* long time."

"It's a matter of five or six years," agreed the charmed Bailey, contemplating her with affectionate pride in her prettiness and grace. "You used to drive out here with your pony and spend many an [33] hour looking on and asking questions. You'll excuse me, Miss Emily, but there was many a man passed the whisper that you'd have made a fine master of the works."

She shook her head, folding her small gloved hands upon the edge of the desk at the opposite sides of which they were seated.

"At least I would have tried. I am quite sure I would have tried. But I am only a girl. I came to ask you something regarding that," she lifted her candid eyes to his, her soft color rising. "Do you know—have you ever met any men who cared and understood about such factories as this? Men who could take charge of a business, the manufacturing and racing and selling, like my uncles? I have a reason for asking." [34]

"Sure thing," said Bailey, unexpectedly prompt. "I've met one man who knows how to handle this factory better than I do, and I've been at it twelve years. And there he is—" he turned in his revolving chair and rolled up the shade covering the glass-set door into the next room, "my manager, Lestrange."

The scene thus suddenly opened to the startled Emily was sufficiently matter-of-fact, yet not lacking in a certain sober animation of its own. Around a drafting table central in the bare, systematic disorder of the apartment beyond, three or four blue-shirted men were grouped, bending over a set of drawings, which Lestrange was explaining. Explaining with a vivid interest in his task that sparkled over his clear face in a changing play of expression almost mesmeric in its com [35] mand of attention. The men watched and listened intently; they themselves no common laborers, but the intelligent workmen who were to carry out the ideas here set forth. Wherever Lestrange had been, he was coatless and the sleeves of his outing shirt were rolled back, leaving bare the arms whose smooth symmetry revealed little of the racing driver's strength; his thick brown hair was rumpled into boyish waves and across his forehead a fine black streak wrote of recent personal encounter with things practical.

"Oh!" exclaimed Emily faintly. And after a moment, "Close the curtain, please."

None of the group in the next room had noticed the movement of the shade, absorbed in one another; any sound being [36] muffled by the throb of adjacent machinery. Bailey obeyed the request, and leaned back in his chair.

"That's Darling Lestrange," he stated with satisfaction. "That's his own design for an oiling system he's busy with, and it's a beauty. He's entered for every big race coming this season, starting next week in Georgia, and meantime he oversees every department in every building as it never was done before. The man for me, he is."

Emily made an unenthusiastic sign of agreement.

"I meant very different men from Mr. Lestrange," she replied, her dignity altogether Ffrench. "I have no doubt that he is all you say, but I was thinking of another class. I meant—well, I meant a gentleman." [37]

"Oh, you meant a gentleman," replied Bailey, surveying her oddly. "I didn't know, you see. No; I don't know any one like that."

"Thank you. Then I will go. I—it does not matter."

She did not go, however, but remained leaning on the arm of her chair in troubled reverie, her long lashes lowered. Bailey sat as quietly, watching her and waiting.

The murmur of voices came dully through the closed door, one, lighter and clearer in tone, most frequently rising above the roar pervading the whole building. It was not possible that Emily's glimpse of Lestrange across the glass should identify him absolutely with the man she had seen once in the flickering lights and shadows on the Long Island [38] road; but he was not of a type easily forgotten, and she had been awakened to a doubting recognition.

Now, many little circumstances recurred to her; a strangeness in Dick's manner when the new manager was alluded to, the fact that her rescuer on that October night had been driving a racing car and had worn a racing costume; and lastly, when Bailey spoke of "Darling" Lestrange there had flashed across her mind the mechanician's ridiculous answer to the request to aid her chauffeur in changing a tire: "I'll do it for you, Darling." And listening to that dominant voice in the next room, she slowly grew crimson before a vision of herself in the middle of a country road, appealing to a stranger for succor, like the heroine of melodramatic fiction. Decid [39] edly, she would never see Lestrange, never let him discover Miss Ffrench.

"I will go," she reiterated, rising impetuously.

The glass-set door opened with unwarning abruptness.

"I'll see Mr. Bailey," declared some one. "He'll know."

Helpless, Emily stood still, and straightway found herself looking directly into Lestrange's gray eyes as he halted on the threshold.

It was Bailey who upheld the moment, all unconsciously.

"Come in," he invited heartily. "Miss Ffrench, this is our manager, Mr. Lestrange; the man who's going to double our sales this year."

Emily moved, then straightened herself proudly, lifting her small head. Le [40] strange had recognized her, she felt; the call was to courage, not flight.

"I think I have already met Mr. Lestrange," she said composedly. "I am pleased to meet him again."

"Met him!" cried Bailey. "Met him? Why—"

Neither heeded him. A gleaming surprise and warmth lit Lestrange's always brilliant face.

"Thank you," he answered her. "You are more than good to recall me, Miss Ffrench. I owe an apology for breaking in this way, but I fancied Mr. Bailey alone—and he spoils me."

"It is nothing; I was about to go." She turned to give Bailey her hand, smiling involuntarily in her relief. With a glance, an inflection, Lestrange had stripped their former meeting of its em [41] barrassment and unconventionality, how, she neither analyzed nor cared.

"Good morning," said Bailey. "Shall I take you through, or—"

But Lestrange was already holding open the door, with a bright unconcern as to his workmanlike costume which impressed Emily pleasantly. She wondered if Dick would have borne the situation as well, in the impossible event of his being found at work.

The two walked together down an aisle of the huge, machinery-crowded room, the grimy men lifting their heads to gaze after Emily as she passed. Once Lestrange paused to speak to a man who sat, note-book and pencil in hand, beside another who manipulated under a grinding wheel a delicate aluminum casting.

"Pardon," he apologized to Emily, [42] who had lingered also. "Mathews would have let that go wrong in another moment. He," his smile glanced out, "he is not a Rupert at changing his tires, so to speak, but just a good chauffeur."

The gay and natural allusion delighted her. For the first time in her life Emily Ffrench laughed out in a genuine, mischievous sense of adventure.

"Yes? I wonder you could separate yourself from that Rupert to come here; he was a most bewildering person," she retorted.

"Separate from Rupert? Why, I would not think of racing a taxi-cab, as he would say, without Rupert beside me. He is here taking a post-graduate course in this type of car, in order to be up to his work when we go down to Georgia next week." [43]

"Next week? You expect to win that race?"

"No. We are running a stock car against some heavy foreign racing machines; the chance of winning is slight. But I hope to outrun any other American car on the course, if nothing goes wrong."

She looked up.

"And if something does?" she wondered.

He shrugged his shoulders.

"Pray be careful of those moving belts behind you, Miss Ffrench. If something does—there is a chance in every game worth playing."

"A chance!" her feminine nerves recoiled from the implied consequences. "But only a chance, surely. You were never in an accident, never were hurt?" [44]

Lestrange regarded her in surprise mingled with a dawning raillery infinitely indulgent.

"I had no accidents last season," he guardedly responded. "I've been quite lucky. At least Rupert and I play our game unhampered; there will be no broken hearts if we are picked up from under our car some day."

They had reached the door while he spoke; as he put his hand on the knob to open it, Emily saw a long zigzag scar running up the extended arm from wrist to elbow, a mute commentary on the conversation. In silence she passed out across the courtyard to where her red-wheeled cart waited. But when Lestrange had put her in and given her the reins, she held out her hand to him with more gravity. [45]

"I shall wish you good luck for next week," she said.

Lestrange threw back his head, drawing a quick breath; here in the strong sunlight he showed even younger than she had thought him, young with a primitive intensity of just being alive.

"Thank you. I would like—if it were possible—to win this race."

"This one, especially?"

"Yes, because it is the next step toward a purpose I have set my-self, and which I shall accomplish if I live. Not that I will halt if this step fails, no, nor for a score of such failures, but I am anxious to go on and finish."

Up to Emily's face rushed the answering color and fire to his; drawn by the bond of mutual earnestness, she leaned nearer. [46]

"You live to do something? So do I, so do I! And every one else *plays*."

However Lestrange would have replied, he was checked by the crash of the courtyard gate. Abruptly recalled to herself, Emily turned, to see Dick Ffrench coming toward them.

Remembering how the three had last met, the situation suggested strain. But to Emily's astonishment the young men exchanged friendly nods, although Dick flushed pink.

"Good morning, Lestrange," he greeted. "I've just come up from the city, Emily, and there wasn't any carriage at the station, so when one of the testers told me you were here I came over to get a ride."

"I've been to see Mr. Bailey," she responded. "Get in." [47]

As Dick climbed in beside her, she bent her head to Lestrange; if she had regretted her impulsive confidence, again the clear sanity and calm of the gray eyes she encountered established self-content.

When they were trotting down the road toward home, in the crisp air, Emily glanced at her cousin.

"I did not know you and Mr. Lestrange were so well acquainted," she remarked.

"I see him now and then," Dick answered uneasily. "He's too busy to want me bothering around him much. You — remembered him?"

"Yes."

He absently took the whip from its socket, flecking the horse with it as he spoke.

"It was awfully square of you, Emily, not to mention that night to Uncle Ethan. [48] It wasn't like a girl, at all. I made an idiot of my-self, and you've never said anything to me about it since. I never told you where Lestrange took me, because I didn't like to talk of the thing. I'm really awfully fond of you, cousin."

"Yes, Dickie," she said patiently.

"Well, Lestrange rubbed it in. Oh, he didn't say much. But he carried me down to where they were practising for a road race. Such a jolly lot of fellows, like a bunch of kids; teasing and calling jokes back and forth at one another half the night until daybreak, everything raw and chilly. Busy, and their mechanics busy, and one after another swinging into his car and going off like a rocket. By the time Lestrange went off, I was as much stirred up as anybody. When he made a record circuit at seventy-seven [49] miles an hour average, I was shouting over the rail like a good one. And then, while he was off again, a big blue car rolled in and its driver yelled that Lestrange had gone over on the Eastbury turn, and to send around the ambulance. It was like a nightmare; I sat down on a stone and felt sick."

"He—"

"He shook me up half an hour later, and stood laughing at me. 'Upset?' he said. 'No; we shed a tire and went off into a field, but it didn't hurt the machine, so we righted her and came in.' He was limping and bruised and scratched, but he was laughing, while a crowd of people were trying to shake hands with him and say things. I felt—funny; as if I wasn't much good. I never felt like that before. 'This is only practise,' he said, when I [50] was about to go. 'The race to-morrow will do better. We find it more exciting than cocktails.' That was all, but I knew what he meant, all right. I've been careful ever since. He won the race next day, too."

"Dick, didn't it ever occur to you that you as well as Mr. Lestrange might do real things?" she asked, after a moment.

He turned his round, good-humored face to her in boundless amazement.

"I? I race cars and break my neck and call it fun, like Lestrange? You're laughing at me, Emily."

"No, no," in spite of herself the picture evoked brought her smile. "Not like that. But you might be interested in the factory. You might learn from Mr. Bailey and take charge of the business with Uncle

Ethan. It would please [51] uncle, *how* it would please him, if you did!"

Dick stirred unhappily.

"It would take a lot of grind," he objected. "I haven't the head for it, really. I'm not such an awfully bad lot, but I hate work. Let's not be serious, cousin. How pretty the frosty wind makes you look!"

Emily tightened the reins with a brief sigh of resignation.

"Never mind, Dickie. I—uncle will find a substitute. Things must go on somehow, I suppose, even if we do not like the way."

But the way loomed distasteful that morning as never before.

[52]

IV

M

r. Ffrench and his niece were at breakfast, on the Sunday when the first account of the Georgia race reached Ffrenchwood.

"You will take fresh coffee," Emily was saying, the little silver pot poised in her hand, when the door burst open and Dick hurried, actually hurried, into the room.

"He's won! He's got it!" he cried, brandishing the morning newspaper. "The first time for an American car with an American driver. And how he won it! He distanced every car on the track except the two big Italian and French machines. Those he couldn't get, of course; but the Frenchman went out in [53] the fourth hour with a broken valve. Then he was set down for second place—second place, Emily, with every other big car in the country entered. They say he drove like, like—I don't know what. A hundred and some miles an hour on the straight stretches."

"Oh," Emily faltered, setting down the coffee-pot in her plate.

He stopped her eagerly, half turning toward Mr. Ffrench, who had put on his pince-nez to contemplate his nephew in stupefaction, not at his statement, but at his condition.

"Wait. In the last hour, the Italian car lost its chain and went over into a ditch on a back stretch, three miles from a doctor. People

36

around picked the men out of the wreck, and Lestrange came up to find that the driver was likely to die [54] from a severed artery before help got there. Emily, he stopped, stopped, with victory in his hands, had the Italian lifted into the mechanician's seat, and Rupert held him in while they dashed around the course to the hospital. He got him there fifteen minutes before an ambulance could have reached him, and the man will get well. But Lestrange had lost six minutes. He had rushed straight to the doctor's, given them the man, and gone right on, but he had lost six minutes. When people realized what he'd done, they went wild. Every one thought he'd lost the race, but they cheered him until they couldn't shout. And he kept on driving. It's all here," he waved the gaudy sheet. "The paper's full of it. He had half an hour to make up six minutes, and he did it. He came in nine [55] teen seconds ahead of the nearest car. The crowd swarmed out on the course and fell all over him. Old Bailey's nearly crazy."

To see Dick excited would have been marvel enough to hold his auditors mute, if the story itself had not possessed a quality to stir even non-sporting blood. Emily could only sit and gaze at the headlines of the extended newspaper, her dark eyes wide and shining, her soft lips apart.

"He telegraphed to Bailey," Dick added, in the pause. "Ten words: 'First across line in Georgia race. Car in fine shape. Lestrange.' That was all."

Mr. Ffrench deliberately passed his coffee-cup to Emily.

"You had better take your breakfast," he advised. "It is unusual to see you noticing business affairs, Dick; I might [56] say unprecedented. I am glad if Bailey's new man is capable of his work, at least. I suppose for the rest, that he could scarcely do less than take an injured person to the hospital. Why are you putting sugar in my cup, Emily?"

"I don't know," she acknowledged helplessly.

"I didn't mean to disturb any one," said Dick, sulky and resentful. "It'll be a big thing though for our cars, Bailey says. I didn't know you disliked Lestrange."

Mr. Ffrench stiffened in his chair.

"I have not sufficient interest in the man to dislike him," was the cold rebuke. "We will change the subject."

Emily bent her head, remedying her mistake with the coffee. She comprehended that her uncle had conceived one [57] of his strong, silent antipathies for the young manager, and she was sorry. Sorry, although, remembering Bailey's unfortunate speech the night Lestrange's engagement was proposed, she was not surprised. But she looked across to Dick sympathetically. So sympathetically, that after breakfast he followed her into the library, the colored journals in his hand.

"What's the matter with the old gentleman this morning?" he complained. "He wants the business to succeed, doesn't he? If he does, he ought to like what Lestrange is doing for it. What's the matter with him?"

Emily shook back her yellow curls, turning her gaze on him.

"You might guess, Dickie. He is lonely." [58]

"Lonely! He!"

All the feminine impulse to defend flared up.

"Why not?" she exclaimed with passion. "Who has he got? Who stands with him in his house? No wonder he can not bear the man who is hired to do what a Ffrench should be doing. It is not the racing driver he dislikes, but the manager. And do not you blame him, Dick Ffrench."

Quite aghast, he stared after her as she turned away to the nearest window. But presently he followed her over, still holding the papers.

"Don't you want to read about the race?" he ventured.

Smiling, though her lashes were damp, Emily accepted the peace offering.

"Yes, please." [59]

"You're not angry? You know I'm a stupid chump sometimes; I don't mean it."

This time she laughed outright.

"No; I am sorry I was cross. It is I who would like to shirk my work. Never mind me; let us read."

They did read, seated opposite each other in the broad window-seat and passing the sheets across as they finished them. Dick had not exaggerated, on the contrary he had not said enough. Lestrange and his car were the focus of the hour's attention. The daring, the reckless courage that risked life for victory, the generosity which could throw that victory away to aid a comrade, and lastly the determination and skill which had won the conquest after all—the whole formed a feat too spectacular to escape [60] public hysteria. It was very doubtful indeed whether Lestrange liked his idolizing, but there was no escape.

The two who read were young.

"It was a splendid fight," sighed Dick, when they dropped the last page.

"Yes," Emily assented. "When he comes back, when you see him, give him my congratulations."

"When I see him? Why don't you tell him yourself?"

Something like a white shadow wiped the scarlet of excitement from her cheeks, as she averted her face.

"I shall not see him; I shall not go to the factory any more. It will be better, I am sure."

Vaguely puzzled and dismayed, Dick sat looking at her, not daring to question.

Emily kept her word during the weeks [61] that followed. Through Dick and Bailey she heard of factory affairs; of the sudden increase of orders for the Mercury automobiles, the added prestige gained, and the public favor bestowed on the car. But she saw nothing of the man who was responsible for all this. Instead she went out more than ever before. Their social circle was too painfully exclusive to be large or gay.

Three times a week it was Mr. Ffrench's stately custom to visit the factory and inspect it with Bailey. At other times Bailey came up to the house, where affairs were conducted. But in neither place did

Mr. Ffrench ever come in contact with his manager, during all the months while winter waxed and waned again to spring.

"That's Bailey's doing," chuckled [62] Dick, when Emily finally wondered aloud at the circumstance. "He isn't going to risk losing Lestrange because our high and mighty uncle falls out with him. And it would be pretty likely to happen if they met. Lestrange has a temper, you know, even if it doesn't stick out all over him like a hedgehog; and a dozen other companies would give money to get him."

Emily nodded gravely. It was a sunny morning in the first of March, and the cousins were at the end of the old park surrounding Ffrenchwood, where they had strolled before breakfast.

"Mr. Bailey likes Mr. Lestrange," she commented.

"Likes him! He loves him. You know Lestrange lives with him; a bachelor household, cozy as grigs." [63]

Just past here ran the road, beyond a high cedar hedge. While he was speaking, the irregular explosive reports of a motor had sounded down the valley, unmistakable to those familiar with the testing of the stripped cars, and rapidly approaching. Now, as Emily would have answered, the roar suddenly changed in character, an appalling series of explosions mingled with the grind of outraged machinery suddenly braked, and some one shouted above the din. The next instant a huge mass shot past the other side of the hedge and there followed a dull crash.

"That's one of our men!" gasped Dick, and plunged headlong through the shrubbery.

Dazed momentarily, Emily stood, then caught up her skirts and ran after him. [64] She knew well enough what the testers of the cars risked.

"Dick!" she appealed. "Dick!"

But it was not the wreck she anticipated that met her eyes as she came through the hedge. On the opposite side of the road a long low skeleton car was standing, one side lurched drunkenly down with two wheels in the gutter. Still in his seat, the driver was leaning over the steering-wheel, out of breath, but laughing a greeting to the astonished Dick.

"A break in the steering-gear," he declared, by way of explanation. "I told Bailey it was a weak point; now perhaps he'll believe me and strengthen it."

"You're not hurt," Dick inferred.

"I think she's not—a tire gone. Find anything wrong, Rupert?"

"Two tires off," said the laconic me [65] chanician. "Two funerals postponed. That was a pretty stop, Darling."

"Very," coolly agreed Lestrange, rising and removing his goggles. "What's the matter, Ffrench?"

"You frightened us out of our five senses, that's all. Do you usually practise for races out here?"

"*Us?*" repeated Lestrange, and turning, saw the girl at the edge of the park. "Miss Ffrench, I beg your pardon!"

The swift change in his tone, the ease of deference with which he bared his head and, motor caps not being readily donned or doffed, so remained bareheaded in the bright sunlight, savored of the Continent.

"It is too commonplace to say good morning," Emily replied, her color rising with her smile. "I am very glad you [66] escaped. But that is commonplace, too, I'm afraid."

"Every one is commonplace before breakfast," reassured her cousin. "Honestly, Lestrange, do you practise racing here?"

"Hardly. I'm trying out the car; every car has to go through that before it is used. Don't you know that we've recently secured from the local authorities a permit to run at any speed over this road between four o'clock and eight in the morning? I thought all the country-side knew that."

"But we have a regiment of men to test cars."

Lestrange passed a caressing glance over the dingy-gray machine in its state of bareness that suggested indecorum.

"This is my car, the one I'll race this [67] spring and summer. No one drives it but me. Besides, I have to have some diversion."

He stepped to the ground with the last word, and went around to where Rupert was on his knees beside the machine.

"Can you fix it here?" he demanded.

"Not precisely," was the drawled reply. "Back to camp for it with a horse in front."

"All right. You'll have to walk down and get a car from Mr. Bailey to tow it home."

Rupert got up, his dark, malign little face twisted.

"If I'd broken a leg they'd have sent a cart for me," he mourned. "Now I'll have to walk, and I ain't used to it. Hard luck!"

"If you go around to the stables they [68] will give you my pony cart," Emily offered impulsively. "You," her dimpling smile gleamed out, "you once put a tire on for me, you know. Please let me return the service."

Rupert's black eyes opened, a slow grin of appreciation crinkled streaks of dust and oil as he surveyed the young girl.

"I'll put tires on every wheel you run into control, day and night shifts," he acknowledged with sweet cordiality. "But I'm no horse-chauffeur, thanks; I guess I'll walk."

"He is a gentle pony," she remonstrated. "Any one can drive him."

He turned a side glance toward the motionless car.

"That's all right, but I'm used to being killed other ways. I'll be going."

"Jack Rupert, do you mean to tell me [69] that you will race with Lestrange every season, and yet you're afraid to drive a fat cob?" cried the delighted Dick.

"I'm not telling anything. I had a chum who was pitched out by a horse he lost control of, and broke his neck. I'm taking no chances."

"How many men have you seen break their necks out of autos?"

"That's in business," pronounced Rupert succinctly. "I'm going on, Darling; it's only a two-mile run."

"Here, wait," Dick urged. "Emily, I'll stroll around to the stables with him and make one of the men drive him down. You don't mind my leaving you?"

"No," Emily answered. "I will wait for you."

She might have walked back alone, if she had chosen. But instead she sat [70] down on a boulder near the hedge, folding her hands in her lap like a demure child. The house was so dull, so hopelessly monotonous contrasted with this fresh, wind-tossed outdoors and Lestrange in his vigor of life and glamour of ultramodern adventure.

"You and Mr. Ffrench are very good," Lestrange said presently. "I am afraid I appreciate it more than Rupert, though."

"Is he really afraid of horses?"

"I should not wonder; I never tried him. But he is amazingly truthful."

Their eyes met across the strip of sunny road as they smiled; again Emily felt the sudden confidence, the falling away of all constraint before the direct clarity of his regard.

"You won your race," she said irrele [71] vantly. "I was glad, since you wanted it."

"Thank you," he returned with equal simplicity. "But I did not want it that way, so far as I was concerned."

"Yet, it was the next step?"

"Yes, it was the next step. I meant that one does not care to be victor because the leading cars were wrecked. There is no elation in defeating a driver who lies out on the course. But, as you say, it helped my purpose. You," he hesitated for the right phrase, "you are most kind to recall that I have a purpose."

It was the convent-bred Emily who looked back at him, earnest-eyed, exaltedly serious.

"I have thought of it often. Every one else that I know just lives the way things happen — there are only a few peo [72] ple who grasp things and *make* them happen. That is real work; so many of us are just given work we do not want — " she broke off.

"If we do not want the work, it is probably not our own," said Lestrange. "Unless we have brought it on ourselves by a fault we must undo — I need not speak of that to you. One must not make the mistake of assuming some one else's work."

He spoke gently, almost as if with a clairvoyant reading of her tendency to self-immolation.

"But may not some one else's fault be given us to undo?" she asked eagerly. "May not their work be forced on us?"

"No," he answered.

"No?" bewildered.

"I don't think so. Each one of us has [73] enough with his own, at least so it seems to me. Most of us die before we finish it."

Emily paused, contending with the loneliness and doubts which impelled her to speech, the feminine yearning to let another decide her problems. This other's nonchalant strength of decision allured her uncertainty.

"I am discouraged," she confessed. "And tired. I — there is no reason why I should not speak of it. You know Dick, how he can do nothing in the factory or business, or in the places where a Ffrench should stand. All this must fall into the hands of strangers, to be broken and forgotten, when my uncle dies, for lack of some one who would care. And Uncle Ethan seems severe and hard, but it grieves him all the time. His only [74] son was not a good man; he lives abroad with his wife, who was an actress before he married her. You knew that?" as he moved.

"I heard something of it in the village," Lestrange admitted gravely. "Please do not think me fond of gossip; I could not avoid it. But I should not have imagined this a family likely to make low marriages."

"It never happened before. I never saw that cousin, nor did Dick; but he was always a disappointment, always, Uncle Ethan has told me. And since he failed, and Dick fails, there is only me."

"You!"

She nodded, her lip quivering.

"Only me. Not as a substitute—I am not fit for that—but to find a substitute. [75] I have promised my uncle to marry the first one who is able to be that."

The silence was absolute. Lestrange neither moved nor spoke, gazing down at her bent head with an expression blending many shades.

"It is a duty; there is no one except me," she added. "Only sometimes I grow—to dislike it too much. I am so selfish that sometimes I hope a substitute will never come."

Her voice died away. It was done; she, Emily Ffrench, had deliberately confided to this stranger that which an hour before she would have believed no one could force from her lips in articulate speech. And she neither regretted nor was ashamed, although there was time for full realization before Lestrange answered. [76]

"I did not believe," he said, "that such things could be done. It is nonsense, of course, but such magnificent nonsense! It is the kind of situation, Miss Ffrench, where any man is justified in interfering. I beg you will leave the affair in my hands and think no more of such morbid self-sacrifice."

Stupefied, Emily flung back her head, staring at him.

"In *your* hands?"

"Since there are none better, it appears. Why," his vivid face questioned her full and straightly, "you didn't imagine that any man living could hear what you are doing, and pass on?"

"My uncle knows—"

"Your uncle—is not for me to criticize. But do not ask any other man to let you go on." [77]

Her ideas reeling, she struggled for comprehension.

"You, what could you do?" she marveled. "The substitute — "

"There won't be any substitute," replied Lestrange with perfect coolness. "I shall train Dick Ffrench to do his work."

"You — "

"I can, and I will."

"He can not — "

"Oh, yes, he can; he is just idle and spoiled," the firm lips set more firmly. "He shall take his place. I can handle him."

Emily sat quite helplessly, her eyes black with excitement. Slowly recollection flowed back to her of a change in Dick since his light contact with Lestrange; his avoidance of even occasional [78] high-balls, his awakening interest in the clean sport of the races, and his half-wistful admiration for the virile driver-manager.

"I almost believe you could," she conceded.

"I can," repeated Lestrange. "Only," he openly smiled, "it will be hard on Dickie."

It was the touch needed, the antidote to sentiment. Emily laughed with him, laughed in sheer mischief and relief and leap of youth.

"You will be gentle — poor Dickie!"

"I'll be gentle. He is coming now, I think." He took a step nearer her. "You will leave this in my care, wholly? You will not trouble about — a substitute?"

"I will leave it with you. But you are [79] forgetting your own doctrine; you are taking some one else's work to do."

"Pardon, I am merely making Ffrench do his work. I have seen a little more of him than you perhaps know; I understand what I am undertaking. Moreover, I would forget a great many doctrines to set you free."

"Free?" she echoed; she had the sensation of being suddenly confronted with an open door into the unexpected.

"Free," he quietly reasserted. "Free to live your own life and draw unhampered breath, and to decide the great question when it comes, with thought only of yourself."

She drew back; a prescient dismay fell sharply across her late relief, a panic crossed with strange delight.

"He's off," called Dick, emerging [80] from the park. "I made Anderson take him down with the limousine. At least, Rupert is driving while Anderson sits alongside and holds on; when they came to the turn in the avenue, your precious mechanician took it full speed and then apologized for going so slowly because, as he said, he was an amateur and likely to upset. Is he really a good driver, Lestrange?"

"Pretty fair," returned Lestrange serenely, from his seat on the edge of the ditched machine. "When I'm not using him, he's employed as one of the factory car testers; and when we're racing I give him the wheel if I want to fix anything. However, I'm obliged to that steering-knuckle for breaking here, instead of leaving me to a long wait in the wilds. Come down to the shop to-morrow at six, and [81] Rupert and I will even up by taking you for a run."

"Who; me? You're asking me?"

"Why not? It's exhilarating."

Dick removed his hat and ran his fingers through his hair, gratification and alarm mingling in his expression with somewhat the effect of the small boy who is first invited into a game with his older brother's clique.

"You — er, wouldn't smash me up?" he hesitated.

"I haven't smashed up Rupert or myself, so far. If you feel timid, never mind, of course; I'll take my usual companion."

Dick flushed all over his plump face, the Ffrench blood up at last.

"I was only joking," he hastily explained. "I'll come. It's only that [82] you're so confoundedly reckless sometimes, Lestrange, and — But I'll come."

Lestrange gave his fine, glinting smile as he rose to salute Emily.

"All right. If you don't get down to the factory in time, I'll call for you," he promised.

[83]

V

here was a change in the Ffrench affairs, a lightening of the atmosphere, a vague quickening and stir of healthful cheer in the days that followed. The somber master of the house met it in Bailey's undisguised elation and pride when they discussed the successful business now taxing the factory's resources, met it yet again in Emily's pretty gaiety and content. But most strikingly was he confronted with an alteration in Dick.

It was only a week after his first morning ride with Lestrange, that Dick electrified the company at dinner, by turning down the glass at his plate.

"I've cut out claret, and that sort of [84] thing," he announced. "It's bad for the nerves."

His three companions looked up in complete astonishment. It was Saturday night and by ancient custom Bailey was dining at the house.

"What has happened to you? Have you been attending a revival meeting?" the young man's uncle inquired with sarcasm.

"It's bad for the nerves," repeated Dick. "There isn't any reason why I shouldn't like to do anything other fellows do. Les—that is, none of the men who drive cars ever touch that stuff, and look at their nerve."

Mr. Ffrench contemplated him with the irritation usually produced by the display of ostentatious virtue, but found no comment. Emily gazed at the table, her [85] red mouth curving in spite of all effort at seriousness.

"You're right, Mr. Dick," said Bailey dryly. "Stick to it."

And Dick stuck, without as much as a single lapse. Ffrenchwood saw comparatively little of him, as time went on, the village and factory much. He lost some weight, and acquired a coat of reddish tan.

Emily watched and admired in silence. She had not seen Lestrange again, but it seemed to her that his influence overlay all the life of both house and factory. Sometimes this showed so plainly that she believed Mr. Ffrench must see, must feel the silent force at work. But either he did not see or chose to ignore. And Dick was incautious.

"I'm going to buy one of our roadsters [86] myself," he stated one day. "Can I have it at cost?"

Mr. Ffrench felt for his pince-nez.

"You? Why do you not use the limousine?"

"Because I don't want to go around in a box driven by a chauffeur. I want a classy car to run myself. I've been driving some of the stripped cars, lately, and I like it."

"I will give you a car, if you want one," answered his uncle, quite kindly. "Go select any you prefer."

"Thank you," Dick sat up, beaming. "But I'll have to wait my turn, we've orders ahead now. Lestrange says I've no right to come in and make some other fellow wait."

Mr. Ffrench slowly stiffened.

"We do not require lessons in ethics [87] from this Lestrange," was the cold rebuke. "I shall telephone Bailey to send up your car at once."

Rupert brought the sixty-horse-power roadster to the door, three hours later. And Emily appreciated that Lestrange was discreet as well as compelling, when she found the black-eyed young mechanician was detailed to accompany Dick's maiden trips; which duty was fulfilled, incidentally, with the fine tact of a Richelieu.

In May there was a still greater accession of work at the factory. In addition, the first of June was to open with a twenty-four hour race at the Beach track, and Lestrange was entered for it. Excitement was in the air; Dick came in the house only to eat and sleep.

The day before the race, Mr. Ffrench [88] walked into the room where his niece was reading.

"I want to see Bailey," he said briefly. "Do you wish to drive me down to the factory, or shall I have Anderson bring around the limousine?"

"Please let us drive," she exclaimed, rising with alacrity. "I have not been to the factory for months."

"Very good. You are looking well, Emily, of late."

Surprised, a soft color swept the face she turned to him.

"I am well. Dear, I think we are all better this spring."

"Perhaps," said Ethan Ffrench. His bitter gray eyes passed deliberately over the large room with all its traces of a family life extending back to pre-Colonial times, but he said no more. [89]

It was an exquisite morning, too virginal for June, too richly warm for May. When the two exchanged the sunny road for the factory office, a north room none too light, it was a moment before their dazzled eyes perceived no one was present. This was Bailey's private office, and its owner had passed into the room beyond.

"I will wait," conceded Mr. Ffrench, dismissing the boy who had ushered them in. "Sit down, Emily; Bailey will return directly, no doubt."

But Emily had already sat down, for she knew the voice speaking beyond the half-open door, and that the long-prevented meeting was now imminent.

"It will not do," Lestrange was stating definitely. "It should be reinforced."

"It's always been strong enough," Bai [90] ley's slower tones objected. "For years. It's not a thing likely to break."

"Not likely to break? Look at last year's record, Mr. Bailey, and tell me that. A broken steering-knuckle killed Brook in Indiana, another sent Little to the hospital in Massachusetts, the same thing wrecked the leader at the last Beach race and dashed him through the fence. Do you know what it means to the driver of a machine hurling itself along the narrow verge of destruction, when the steering-wheel suddenly turns useless in his grasp? Can you feel the sick helplessness, the confronting of death, the compressed second before the crash? Is it worth while to risk it for a bit of costless steel?"

The clear realism of the picture forced a pause, filled by the dull roar and throb [91] through the machinery-crowded building.

"They were not our cars that broke, any of them," Bailey insisted.

"Not our cars, no. But the steering-knuckle of my own machine broke under my hands last March, on the road, and if I had been on a curve instead of a straight stretch there would have been a wreck. As it was, I brought her to a stop in the ditch. There is no other thing that may not leave a fighting chance after it breaks, but this leaves absolutely none. I know, you both know, that the steering-wheel is the only weapon in the driver's grasp. If it fails him, he goes out and his mechanician with him."

Emily paled, shrinking. She remembered the road under the maples and Lestrange's laughing face as he leaned [92] breathless across his useless wheel. That was what it had meant, then, the lightly treated episode!

"You'd better fix it like he wants it," advised Dick's disturbed tones. "Remember, he's got to drive the car Friday and Saturday, Bailey, not us."

"It's not alone for my racer I'm speaking, but for every car that leaves the shop," Lestrange caught him up. "I'm not flinching; I've driven the car before and I will again. It may hold for ever, that part, but I've tested it and it's a weak point — take the warning for what it's worth."

There was a movement as if he rose with the last word. Emily laid her hand on the arm of the chair, turning her excited dark eyes on her uncle. Surely if ever Mr. Ffrench was to meet his man [93] ager, this was the moment; when Lestrange's ringing argument was still in their ears, his splendid force of earnestness still vibrant in the atmosphere. And suddenly she wanted them to meet, passionately wanted Ethan Ffrench's liking for this man.

"Uncle," she began. "Uncle — "

But it was not Lestrange's light step that halted on the threshold.

"Why, I didn't know—" exclaimed Bailey. "Excuse me, Mr. Ffrench, they didn't tell me you were down."

He glanced over his shoulder; as he pulled shut the door Emily fancied she heard an echo, as if the two young men left the next room. Bitterly disappointed, she sank back.

"That was your manager with you?" Mr. Ffrench frigidly inquired. [94]

"Yes; he went up-stairs to see how the new drill is acting." Bailey pulled out a handkerchief and rubbed his brow. "Excuse me, it's warm. Yes, he wants me to strengthen a knuckle—he's spoken considerable about it. I guess he's right; better too much than too little."

"I do not see that follows. I should imagine that you understood building chassis better than this racing driver. You had best consult outside experts in construction before making a change."

"Uncle!" Emily cried.

"There's a twenty-four hour race starts to-morrow night," Bailey suggested uneasily. "It's easy fixed, and we might be wrong."

"We have always made them this way?"

"Yes, but—" [95]

"Consult experts, then. I do not like your manager's tone; he is too assuming. Now let me see those papers."

Emily's parasol slipped to the floor with a sharp crash as she stood up, quite pale and shaken.

"Uncle, Mr. Lestrange knows," she appealed. "You heard him say what would happen—please, please let it be fixed."

Amazed, Mr. Ffrench looked at her, his face setting.

"You forget your dignity," he retorted in displeasure. "This is mere childishness, Emily. Men will be consulted more competent to decide than this Lestrange. That will do."

From one to the other she gazed, then turned away.

"I will wait out in the cart," she said. "I—I would rather be outdoors." [96]

Dick Ffrench was up-stairs, standing with Lestrange in one of the narrow aisles between lines of grimly efficient machines that bit or cut their way through the steel and aluminum fed to them, when Rupert came to him with a folded visiting card.

"Miss Ffrench sent it," was the explanation. "She's sitting out in her horse-motor car, and she called me off the track to ask me to demean myself by acting like a messenger boy. All right?"

"All right," said Dick, running an astonished eye over the card.

"No answer?"

"No answer."

"Then I'll hurry back to my embroidery. I'm several laps behind in my work already."

"See here, Lestrange," Dick began, as the mechanician departed, sitting down [97] on a railing beside a machine steadily engaged in notching steel disks into gear-wheels.

"Don't do that!" Lestrange exclaimed sharply. "Get up, Ffrench."

"It's safe enough."

"It's nothing of the kind. The least slip—"

"Oh, well," he reluctantly rose, "if you're going to get fussy. Read what Emily sent up."

Lestrange accepted the card with a faint flicker of expression.

"Dick, uncle is making the steering-knuckle wait for expert opinion," the legend ran, in pencil. "Have Mr. Bailey strengthen Mr. Lestrange's car, anyhow. Do not let him race so."

Near them two men were engaged in babbitting bearings, passing ladlefuls of [98] molten metal carelessly back and forth, and splashing hissing drops over the floor; at them Lestrange gazed in silence, after reading, the card still in his hand.

"Well?" Dick at last queried.

"Have Mr. Bailey do nothing at all," was the deliberate reply. "There is an etiquette of subordination, I believe—this is Mr. Ffrench's factory. I've done my part and we'll think no more of the matter. I may be wrong. But I am more than grateful to Miss Ffrench."

"That's all you're going to do?"

"Yes. I wish you would not sit there."

"I'm tired; I won't fall in, and I want to think. We've been a lot together this spring, Lestrange; I don't like this business about the steering-gear. Do you go down to the Beach to-morrow?"

"To-night. To-morrow I must put in [99] practising on the track. I would have been down to-day if there had not been so much to do here. Are you coming with me, or not until the evening of the start?"

Dick stirred uncomfortably.

"I don't want to come at all, thank you. I saw you race once."

"You had better get used to it," Lestrange quietly advised. "The day may come when there is no one to take your place. This factory will be yours and you will have to look after your own interests. I wish you would come down and represent the company at this race."

"I haven't the head for it."

"I do not agree with you."

Their eyes met in a long regard. Here, in the crowded room of workers, the ceaseless uproar shut in their conver [100] sation with a walled completeness of privacy.

"I'm not sure whether you know it, Lestrange, but you've got me all stirred up since I met you," the younger man confessed plaintively. "You're different from other fellows and you've made me different. I'd rather be around the factory than anywhere else I know, now. But honestly I like you too well to watch you race."

"I want you to come."

"I—"

One of the men with a vessel of white, heaving molten metal was trying to pass through the narrow aisle. Dick broke his sentence to rise in hasty avoidance, and his foot slipped in a puddle of oil on the floor.

It was so brief in happening that only [101] the workman concerned saw the accident. As Dick fell backward, Lestrange sprang forward and caught him, fairly snatching him from the greedy teeth. There was the rending of fabric, a gasping sob from Dick, and reeling from the recoil, Lestrange was sent staggering against a flying emery wheel next in line.

The workman set down his burden with a recklessness endangering further trouble, active too late.

"Mr. Lestrange!" he cried.

But Lestrange had already recovered himself, his right arm crossed with a scorched and bleeding bar where it had touched the glittering wheel, and the two young men were standing opposite each other in safety.

"You are not hurt?" was the first question. [102]

"*I?* I ought to be, but I'm not. Come to a surgeon, Lestrange—Oh, you told me not to sit there!"

Lestrange glanced down at the surface-wound, then quickly back at the two pallid faces.

"Go on to your work, Peters," he directed. "I'm all right." And as the man slowly obeyed, "*Now* will you take my advice and come to the race with me, Ffrench?"

"Race! You'd race with that arm?"

"Yes. Are you coming with me?"

Shaken and tremulous, Dick passed a damp hand across his forehead.

"I think you're mad to stand talking here. Come to the office, for heaven's sake. And, I'd be ground up there, if you hadn't caught me," he looked toward the jaws sullenly shredding and reshred [103] ding a strip of cloth from his sleeve. "I'll do anything you want."

"Will you?" Lestrange flashed quickly. He flung back his head with the resolute setting of expression the other knew so well, his eyes brilliant with a resolve that took no heed of physical discomfort. "Then give me your word that you'll stick to your work here.

That is my fear; that the change in you is just a mood you'll tire of some day. I want you to stand up to your work and not drop out disqualified."

"I will," said Dick, subdued and earnest. "I couldn't help doing it—your arm—"

Lestrange impatiently dragged out his handkerchief and wound it around the cut.

"Go on." [104]

"I can't help keeping on; I couldn't go back now. You've got me awake. No one else ever tried, and I was having a good time. It began with liking you and thinking of all you did, and feeling funny alongside of you." He paused, struggling with Anglo-Saxon shyness. "I'm awfully fond of you, old fellow."

The other's gray eyes warmed and cleared. Smiling, he held out his left hand.

"It's mutual," he assured. "It isn't playing the game to trap you while you are upset like this. But I don't believe you'll be sorry. Come find some one to tie this up for me; I can't have it stiff to-morrow."

But in spite of his professed haste, Lestrange stopped at the head of the stairs and went back to recover some [105] small object lying on the floor beneath a pool of chilling metal. When he rejoined Dick, it was to linger yet a moment to look back across the teeming room.

"It's worth having, all this," he commented, with the first touch of sadness the other ever had seen in him. "Don't throw it away, Ffrench."

There is usually a surgeon within reach of a factory. When Mr. Ffrench passed out to the cart where Emily waited, he passed Dick and the village physician entering. The elder gentleman put on his glasses to survey his nephew's white face.

"An accident?" he inquired.

The casual curiosity was sufficiently exasperating, and Dick's nerves were badly gone.

"Nothing worth mentioning," he [106] snapped. "Just that I nearly fell into the machinery and Lestrange has done up his arm pulling me out. That's all."

And he hurried the doctor on without further parley or excuse.

Lestrange was in the room behind the office, smoking one of Bailey's cigars and listening to that gentleman's vigorous remarks concerning managers who couldn't keep out of their own machinery, the patient not having considered it worth while to explain Dick's share in the mischance. An omission which Dick himself promptly remedied in his anxious contrition.

Later, when the arm was being swathed in white linen, its owner spoke to his companion of the morning:

"I hope you didn't annoy Miss Ffrench with this trifling matter, as you came in." [107]

"I didn't speak to her at all, only to my uncle."

"Very good."

Something in the too-indolent tone roused Dick's usually dormant observation. Startled, he scrutinized Lestrange.

"Is that why you bothered yourself with me?" he stammered. "Is that why—"

"Shut up!" warned Lestrange forcibly and inelegantly. "That isn't tight enough, Doc. You know I'm experienced at this sort of thing, and I'm going to use this arm."

But Dick was not to be silenced in his new enlightenment. When the surgeon momentarily turned away, he leaned nearer, his plump face grim.

"If I brace up, it won't be for Emily, but for you, Darling Lestrange," he whis [108] pered viciously. "She don't want me and I don't want her, that way. I've got over that. And, and—oh, confound it, I'm sorry, old man!"

"Shut up!" said Lestrange again.

But though Dick's very sympathy unconsciously showed the hopeless chasm between the racing driver and Miss Ffrench, the hurt did not cloud the cordial smile Lestrange sent to mitigate his command.

[109]

VI

Emily first heard the full story of the accident that evening, when Dick sat opposite her on the veranda and gave the account in frank anxiety and dejection.

"We're going down to-night on the nine o'clock train," he added in conclusion. "To-morrow morning he'll spend practising on the track, and to-morrow evening at six the race starts. And Lestrange starts crippled because I am a clumsy idiot. He laughs at me, but—he'd do that anyhow."

"Yes," agreed Emily. "He would do that anyhow." Her eyes were wide and terrified, the little hands she clasped in [110] her lap were quite cold. "I wish, I wish he had never come to this place."

"Oh, you do?" Dick said oddly. "Maybe he will, too, before he gets through with us. We're a nasty lot, we Ffrenches; a lot of blue-blooded snobs without any red blood in us. Are you going to say good-by to me? I won't be home until it's over."

She looked at him, across the odorous dusk slowly silvering as the moon rose.

"You are going to be with him?"

Dick smoothed his leggings before standing up, surveying his strict motor costume with a gloomy pride not to be concealed.

"Yes; I'm representing our company. Lestrange might want some backing if any disputes turned up. Uncle Ethan nearly had a fit when Bailey told him [111] what I was going to do; he called me Richard for the first time in my life. I guess I'll be some good yet, if every one except Lestrange did think I was a chump."

"I am very sure you will," she answered gently. "Good-by, Dick; you look very nice."

When he reached the foot of the steps, her voice recalled him, as she stood leaning over the rail.

"Dick, you could not make him give it up, not race this time?"

He stared up at her white figure.

"No, I could not. Don't you suppose I tried?"

"I suppose you did," she admitted, and went back to her seat.

The June night was very quiet. Once a sleepy bird stirred in the honeysuckle [112] vines and chirped through the dark. Far below the throb of a motor passed down the road, dying away again to leave silence. Suddenly Emily Ffrench hid her face on the arm of her chair and the tears overflowed.

There was no consciousness of time while that inarticulate passion of dread spent itself. But it was nearly half an hour later when she started up at the echo of a light step on the gravel path, dashing her handkerchief across her eyes.

It was incredible, but it was true: Lestrange himself was standing before her at the foot of the low stairs, the moonlight glinting across his uncovered bronze head and bright, clear face.

"I beg pardon for trespass, Miss Ffrench," he said, "but your cousin tells me he has been saying a great deal of non [113] sense to you about this race, and that you were so very good as to feel some concern regarding it. Really, I had to run up and set that right; I couldn't leave you to be annoyed by Mr. Ffrench's nerves. Will you forgive me?"

Like sun through a mist his blithe voice cleaved through her distress. Before the tranquil sanity of his regard, her painted terrors suddenly showed as the artificial canvas scenes of a stage, unreal, untrue.

"It was like you to come," she answered, with a shaking sigh that was half sob. "I was frightened, yes."

"There is no cause. A dozen other men take the same chance as Rupert and I; the driver who alternates with me, for instance. This is our life."

"Your arm—"

"Is well enough." He laughed a little. [114] "You will see many a bandaged arm before the twenty-four hours are up; few of us finish without a scratch or strain or blister. This is a man's game, but it's not half so destructive as foot-ball. You wished me good luck for the Georgia race; will you repeat the honor before I go back to Ffrench?"

"I wish you," she said unsteadily, "every kind of success, now and always. You saved Dick to-day—of all else you have done for him and for me I have not words to speak. But it made it harder to bear the thought of your hurt and risk from the hurt, when I knew that I had sent Dick there, who caused it."

Lestrange hesitated, himself troubled. Her soft loveliness in the delicate light that left her eyes unreadable depths of shadow, her timidity and anxiety for his [115] safety, were from their very un-consciousness most dangerous. And while he grasped at self-control, she came still nearer to the head of the steps and held out her small fair hand, mistaking his silence for leave-taking.

"Good night; and I thank you for coming. I am not used to so much consideration."

Her accents were unsure when she would have made them most certain, with her movement the handkerchief fell from her girdle to his feet. Mechanically Lestrange recovered the bit of linen, and felt it lie wet in his fingers. Wet—

"Emily!" he cried abruptly, and sprang the brief step between them.

Her white, terrified face turned to him in the moonlight, but he saw her eyes. And seeing, he kissed her. [116]

The moment left no time for speech. Some one was coming down the drawing-room toward the long windows. Dick's impatient whistle sounded shrilly from the park. Panting, quivering, Emily drew from the embrace and fled within.

She had no doubt of Lestrange, no question of his serious meaning—he had that force of sincerity which made his silence more convincing than the protestations of others. But alone in her room she laid her cheek against the hand his had touched.

"I wish I had died in the convent," she cried to her heart. "I wish I had died before I made him unhappy too."

[117]

VII

Morning found a pale and languid Emily across the breakfast table from Mr. Ffrench. Yet, by a contradiction of the heart, her pride in loving and being loved so overbore the knowledge that only sorrow could result to herself and Lestrange, that her eyes shone wide and lustrous and her lips curved softly.

Mr. Ffrench was almost in high spirits.

"The boy was merely developing," he stated, over his grape-fruit. "I have been unjust to Richard. For two months Bailey has been talking of his interest in the business and attendance at the factory, but I was incredulous. Although I fan [118] cied I observed a change—have you observed a change in him, Emily?"

"Yes," Emily confirmed, "a very great change. He has grown up, at last."

"Ah? I can not express to you how it gratifies me to have a Ffrench representing me in public; have you seen the morning journals?"

"I have just come down-stairs."

He picked up the newspaper beside him and passed across the folded page.

"*All in readiness for Beach Contest,*" the head-lines ran. "*Last big driver to arrive, Lestrange is in Mercury camp with R. Ffrench, representative of Company.*"

And there was a blurred picture of a speeding car with driver and mechanician masked to goblinesque non-identity, with the legend underneath: "*'Darling' Lestrange, [119] in his Mercury on the Georgia course.*"

"Next year I shall make him part owner. It was always my poor brother's desire to have the future name still Ffrench and Ffrench. He was not thinking of Richard then; he had hope of—"

Emily lifted her gaze from the picture, recalled to attention by the break.

"Of?" she echoed vaguely.

"Of one who is unworthy thought. Richard has redeemed our family from extinction; that is at rest." He paused for an instant. "My dear child, when you are married and established, I shall be content."

Her breathing quickened, her courage rose to the call of the moment.

"If Dick is here, if he is instead of a [120] substitute," she said, carefully quiet in manner, "would it matter, since I am only a girl, whom I married, Uncle Ethan?"

The recollection of that evening when Emily had given her promise of aid, stirred under Mr. Ffrench's self-absorbtion. He looked across the table at her colorless, eager face with perhaps his first thought of what that promise might have cost her.

"No," he replied kindly. "It is part of my satisfaction that you are set free to follow your own choice, without thought of utility or fortune. Of course, I need not say provided the man is of your own class and associations. We will fear no more low marriages."

She had known it before, but it was hard to hear the sentence embodied in words. Emily folded her hands over the [121] paper in her lap and the pleasant breakfast-room darkened before her. Mr. Ffrench continued speaking of Dick, unheard.

When the long meal was ended and her uncle withdrew to meet Bailey in the library, Emily escaped outdoors. There was a quaint summer-house part way down the park, an ancient white pavilion standing beside the brook that gurgled by on its way to the Hudson, where the young girl often passed her hours. She went there now, carrying her little work-basket and the newspaper containing the picture of Lestrange.

"I will save it," was her thought. "Perhaps I may find better ones — this does not show his face — but I will have this now. It may be a long time before I see him." [122]

But she sat with the embroidery scissors in her hand, nevertheless, without cutting the reprint. Lestrange would return to the factory, she never doubted, and all would continue as before, except that she must not see him. He would understand that it was not possible for anything else to happen, at least for many years. Perhaps, after Dick was married —

The green and gold beauty of the morning hurt her with the memory of that other sunny morning, when he had so easily taken from her the task she hated and strove to bear. And he had succeeded, how he had succeeded! Who else in the world could have so transformed Dick? Leaning on the table, her round chin in her palm as she gazed down at the paper in her lap, her fancy slipped [123] back to that night on the Long Island road, when she had first seen his serene genius for setting all things right. How like him that elimination of Dick, instead of a romantic and impracticable attempt to escort her himself.

A bush crackled stiffly at some one's passage; a shadow fell across her.

"Caught!" laughed Lestrange's glad, exultant voice. "Since you look at the portrait, how shall the original fear to present himself? See, I can match." He held out a card burned at the corners and streaked with dull red, "The first time I saw your writing, and found my own name there."

Amazed, Emily sat up, and met in his glowing face all incarnate joy of life and youth.

"Oh!" she gasped piteously. [124]

"You are surprised that I am here? My dear, my dear, after last night did you think I could be anywhere else?"

"The race — "

"I know that track too well to need much practise, and I had the machine out at dawn. My partner is busy practising this morning, and I'll be back in a couple of hours. I was afraid," the gray eyes were so gentle in their brilliancy, "I was afraid you might worry, Emily."

Serenely he assumed possession of her, and the assumption was very sweet. He had not touched her, yet Emily had the sensation of brutally thrusting him away when she spoke:

"How could I do anything else," she asked with desolation, "since we must never meet each other any more? Only, you will not go far away—you will stay [125] where I can sometimes see you as we pass? I—I think I could not bear it to have you go away."

"Emily!"

The scissors clinked sharply to the floor as she held out her white hands in deprecation of his cry; the tears rushed to her eyes.

"You know, you know! I am not free; I am Emily Ffrench. I can not fail my uncle and grieve him as his son did. Oh, I will never marry any one else, and we will hear of each other; I can read in the papers and Dick will tell me of you. It will be something to be so close, down there and up here."

"Emily!"

"You are not angry? You will not be angry? You know I can do nothing else, please say you know." [126]

He came nearer and took both cold little hands in his clasp, bending to her the shining gravity of his regard.

"Did you think me such a selfish animal, my dear, that I would have kissed you when I could not claim you?" he asked. "Did you think I could forget you were Emily Ffrench; even by moonlight?"

Her fair head fell back, her dark eyes questioned his.

"You—mean—"

"I mean that even your uncle can not deny my inherited quality of gentleman. I am no millionaire incognito. I have driven racing cars and managed this factory to earn my living, having no other dependence than upon myself, but my blood is as old as yours, little girl, if that means anything." [127]

"Not to me," she cried, looking up into his eyes. "Not to me, but to him. I cared for *you*—"

He drew her toward him, unresisting, their gaze still on each other. As from the first, there was no shyness between them, but the strange, exquisite understanding now made perfect.

"I was right to come to you," he declared, after a time. "Right to fear that you were troubled, conscientious lady. But I must go back, or there will be a fine disturbance at the Beach. And I have shattered my other plans to insignificant fragments, or you have. If I did not forget by moonlight that you were Emily Ffrench, I certainly forgot everything else."

She looked up at him, her softly tinted face bright as his own, her yellow hair [128] rumpled into flossy tendrils under the black velvet ribbon binding it.

"Everything else?" she echoed. "Is there anything else but this?"

"Nothing that counts, to me. You for my own, and this good world to live in—I stand bareheaded before it all. But yet, I told you once that I had a purpose to accomplish; a purpose now very near completion. In a few months I meant to leave Ffrenchwood."

Emily gave a faint cry.

"Yes, for my work would have been done. Then I fell in love and upset everything. When I tell Mr. Ffrench that I want you, I will have to leave at once."

"Why? You said—"

"How brave are you, Emily?" he asked. "I said your uncle could not [129] question my name or birth, but I did not say he would want to give you to me. Nor will he; unless I am mistaken. Are you going to be brave enough to come to me, knowing he has no right to complain, since you and I together have given him Dick?"

"He does not know you; how can you tell he does not like you?" she urged.

"Do you think he likes 'Darling' Lestrange of the race course?"

The sudden keen demand disconcerted her.

"I hear a little down there," he added. "I have not been fortunate with your kinsman. No, it is for you to say whether Ethan Ffrench's unjust caprice is a bar between us. To me it is none."

"I thought there was to be no more trouble," she faltered, distressed. [130]

Lestrange looked down at her steadily, his gray eyes darkening to an expression she had never seen.

"Have I no right?" was his question. "Is there no cancelling of a claim, is there no subsequent freedom? Is it all no use, Emily?"

Vaguely awed and frightened, her fingers tightened on his arm in a panic of surrender.

"I will come to you, I will come! You know best what is right—I trust you to tell me. Forgive me, dear, I wanted to—"

He silenced her, all the light flashing back to his face.

"A promise; hush! Oh, I shall win to-night with that singing in my ears. I have more to say to you, but not now. I must see Bailey, somehow, before I go." [131]

"He is at the house; let me send him here to you."

"If you come back with him."

They laughed together.

"I will—Do you know," her color deepened rosily, "they all call you 'Darling'; I have never heard your own name."

"My name is David," Lestrange said quietly, and kissed her for farewell.

The earth danced under Emily's feet as she ran across the lawns, the sun glowed warm, the brook tinkled over the cascades in a very madness of mirth. At the head of the veranda steps she turned to look once more at the roof of the white pavilion among the locust trees.

"Uncle will like you when he knows you," she laughed in her heart. "Any one *must* like you." [132]

The servant she met in the hall said that Mr. Bailey had gone out, and Mr. Ffrench also, but separately, the former having taken the short route across toward the factory. That way Emily went in pursuit, intending to overtake him with her pony cart.

But upon reaching the stables, past which the path ran, she found Bailey himself engaged in an inspection of the limousine in company with the chauffeur.

"You'll have to look into her differential, Anderson," he was pronouncing, when the young girl came beside him.

"Come, please," she urged breathlessly.

"Come?" repeated Bailey, wheeling, with his slow benevolent smile. "Sure, Miss Emily; where?"

She shook her head, not replying until they were safely outside; then: [133]

"To Mr. Lestrange; he is in the pavilion. He wants to see you."

"To Lestrange!" he almost shouted, halting. "Lestrange, here?"

"Yes. There is time; he says there is time. He is going back as soon as he sees you."

"But what's he doing here? What does he mean by risking his neck without any practice?"

"He came to see me," she whispered, and stood confessed.

"God!" said Bailey, quite reverently, after a moment of speechless stupefaction. "You, and him!"

She lifted confiding eyes to him, moving nearer.

"It is a secret, but I wanted you to know because you like us both. Dick said you loved Mr. Lestrange." [134]

"Yes," was the dazed assent.

"Well, then—But come, he is waiting."

She was sufficiently unlike the usual Miss Ffrench to bewilder any one. Bailey dumbly followed her back across the park, carrying his hat in his hand.

A short distance from the pavilion Emily stopped abruptly, turning a startled face to her companion.

"Some one is there," she said. "Some one is speaking. I forgot that Uncle Ethan had gone out."

She heard Bailey catch his breath oddly. Her own pulses began to beat with heavy irregularity, as a few steps farther brought the two opposite the open arcade. There they halted, frozen.

In the place Emily had left, where all her feminine toys still lay, Mr. Ffrench [135] was seated as one exhausted by the force of overmastering emotion; his hands clenched on the arms of the chair, his face drawn with passion. Opposite him stood Lestrange, colorless and still as Emily had never conceived him, listening in absolute silence to the bitter address pouring from the other's lips with a low-toned violence indescribable.

"I told you then, never again to come here," first fell upon Emily's conscious hearing. "I supposed you were at least Ffrench enough to take a dismissal. What do you want here, money? I warned you to live upon the allowance sent every month to your bankers, for I would pay no more even to escape the intolerable disgrace of your presence here. Did you imagine me so deserted that I would accept even you as a successor? [136] Wrong; you are not missed. My nephew Richard takes your place, and is fit to take it. Go back to Europe and your low-born wife; there is no lack in my household."

The voice broke in an excess of savage triumph, and Lestrange took the pause without movement or gesture.

"I am going, sir, and I shall never come back," he answered, never more quietly. "I can take a dismissal, yes. If ever I have wished peace or hoped for an accord that never existed between us, I go cured of such folly. But hear this much, since I am arraigned at your bar: I have never yet disgraced your name or mine unless by the boy's mischief which sent me from college. The money you speak of, I have never used; ask Bailey [137] of it, if you will." He hesitated, and in the empty moment there came across the mile of June air the roaring noon whistle of the factory. Involuntarily he turned his head toward the call, but as instantly recovered himself from the self-betrayal. "There is another matter to be arranged, but there is no time now. Nor even in concluding it will I come here again, sir."

There was that in his bearing, in the dignified carefulness of courtesy with which he saluted the other before turning to go, that checked even Ethan Ffrench. But as Lestrange crossed the threshold of the little building, Emily ran from the thicket to meet him, her eyes a dark splendor in her white face, her hands outstretched. [138]

"Not like this!" she panted. "Not without seeing me! Oh, I might have guessed—"

His vivid color and animation returned as he caught her to him, heedless of witnesses.

"You dare? My dear, my dear, not even a question? There is no one like you. Say, shall I take you now, or send Dick for you after the race?"

Mr. Ffrench exclaimed some inarticulate words, but neither heard him.

"Send Dick," Emily answered, her eyes on the gray eyes above her. "Send Dick—I understand, I will come."

He kissed her once, then she drew back and he went down the terraces toward the gates. As Emily sank down on the bench by the pavilion door, Bailey brushed past her, running after the [139] straight, lithe figure that went steadily on out of sight among the huge trees planted and tended by five generations of Ffrenches.

When the vistas of the park were empty, Emily slowly turned to face her uncle.

"You love David Ffrench?" he asked, his voice thin and harsh.

"Yes," she answered. She had no need to ask if Lestrange were meant.

"He is married to some woman of the music-halls."

"No."

"How do you know? He has told you?"

She lifted to him the superb confidence of her glance, although nervous tremors shook her in wavelike succession.

"If he had been married, he would not [140] have made me care for him. He has asked me to be his wife."

They were equally strange to each other in these new characters, and equally spent by emotion. Neither moving, they sat opposite each other in silence. So Bailey found them when he came back later, to take his massive stand in the doorway, his hands in his pockets and his strong jaw set.

"I think that things are kind of mixed up here, Mr. Ffrench," he stated grimly. "I guess I'm the one to straighten them out a bit; I've loved Mr. David from the time he was a kid and never saw him get a square deal yet. You asked him what he was doing here—I'll tell you; he is Lestrange."

There is a degree of amazement which [141] precludes speech; Mr. Ffrench looked back at his partner, mute.

"He is Lestrange. He never meant you to know; he'd have left without your ever knowing, but for Miss Emily. I guess I don't need to remind you of what he's done; if it hadn't been for him we might have closed our doors some day. He understands the business as none of us back-number, old-fashioned ones do; he took hold and shook some life into it. We can make cars, but he can make people buy them. Advertising! Why, just that fool picture he drew on the back of a pad, one day, of a row of thermometers up to one hundred forty, with the sign 'Mercuries are at the top,' made more people notice."

Bailey cleared his throat. "He was al [142] ways making people notice, and laughing while he did it. He's risked his neck on every course going, to bring our cars in first, he's lent his fame as a racing driver to help us along. And now everything is fixed the way we want, he's thrown out. What did he do it for? He thought he needed to square accounts with you, for being born, I suppose; so when he heard how things were going with us he came to me and offered his help. At least, that's what he said. I believe he came because he couldn't bear to see the place go under."

There was a skein of blue silk swinging over the edge of the table. Mr. Ffrench picked it up and replaced it in Emily's work-basket before replying.

70

"If this remarkable story is true," he began, accurately precise in accent. [143]

"You don't need me to tell you it is," retorted Bailey. "You know what my new manager's been doing; why, you disliked him without seeing him, but you had to admit his good work. And I heard you talking about his allowance, Mr. Ffrench. He never touched it, not from the first; it piled up for six years. Last April, when we needed cash in a hurry, he drew it out and gave it to me to buy aluminum. When he left here first he drove a taxicab in New York City until he got into racing work and made Darling Lestrange famous all over the continent. I guess it went pretty hard for a while; if he'd been the things you called him, he'd have gone to the devil alone in New York. But, he didn't."

An oriole darted in one arcade and out again with a musical whir of wings. The [144] clink of glass and silver sounded from the house windows with a pleasant cheeriness and suggestion of comfort and plenty.

"He made good," Bailey concluded thoughtfully. "But it sounded queer to me to hear you tell him you didn't want him around because Mr. Dick took his place. I know, and Miss Emily knows, that Dick Ffrench was no use on earth for any place until Mr. David took him in hand and made him fit to live. That's all, I guess, that I had to say; I'll get back to work." He turned, but paused to glance around. "It's going to be pretty dull at the factory for me. And between us we've sent Lestrange to the track with a nice set of nerves."

His retreating footsteps died away to leave the noon hush unbroken. As before [145] fore, uncle and niece were left opposite each other, the crumpled newspaper where Lestrange's name showed in heavy type still lying on the floor between them.

The effect of Bailey's final sentence had been to leave Emily dizzied by apprehension. But when Mr. Ffrench rose and passed out, she aroused to look up at him eagerly.

"Uncle," she faltered.

Disregarding or unseeing her outstretched hand, he went on and left her there alone. And then Emily dared rescue the newspaper.

"A substitute," she whispered. "A substitute," and laid her wet cheek against the pictured driver.

No one lunched at the Ffrench home that day, except the servants. Near three o'clock in the afternoon Mr. Ffrench [146] came back to the pavilion where Emily still sat.

"Go change your gown," he commanded, in his usual tone. "We will start now. I have sent for Bailey and ordered Anderson to bring the automobile."

"Start?" she wondered, bewildered.

He met her gaze with a stately repellence of comment.

"For the Beach. I understand this race lasts twenty-four hours. Have you any objection?"

Objection to being near David! Emily sprang to her feet.

[147]

VIII

S ix o'clock was the hour set for the start of the Beach race. And it was just seventeen minutes past five when Dick Ffrench, hanging in a frenzy of anxiety over the paddock fence circling the inside of the mile oval, uttered something resembling a howl and rushed to the gate to signal his recreant driver. From the opposite side of the track Lestrange waved gay return, making his way through the officials and friends who pressed around him to shake hands or slap his shoulder caressingly, jesting and questioning, calling directions and advice. A brass band played noisily in the grand-stand, where the crowd [148] heaved and surged; the racing machines were roaring in their camps.

"What's the matter? Where were you?" cried Dick, when at last Lestrange crossed the course to the central field. "The cars are going out now for the preliminary run. Rupert's nearly crazy, snarling at everybody, and the other man has been getting ready to start instead of you."

"Well, he can get unready," smiled Lestrange. "Keep cool, Ffrench; I've got half an hour and I could start now. I'm ready."

He was ready; clad in the close-fitting khaki costume whose immaculate daintiness gave no hint of the certainty that before the first six hours ended it would be a wreck of yellow dust and oil. As he paused in running an appraising [149] glance down the street-like row of tents, the white-clothed driver of a spotless white car shot out on his way to the track, but halted opposite the latest arrival to stretch down a cordial hand.

"I hoped a trolley-car had bitten you," he shouted. "The rest of us would have more show if you got lost on the way, Darling."

The boyish driver at the next tent looked up as they passed, and came over grinning to give his clasp.

"Get a move on; what you been doin' all day, dear child? They've been givin' your manager sal volatile to hold him still." He nodded at the agitated Dick in ironic commiseration.

"Go get out your car, Darling; I want to beat you," chaffed the next in line.

"'Strike up the band, here comes a [150] driver,'" sang another, with an entrancing French accent.

Laughing, retorting, shaking hands with each comrade rival, Lestrange went down the row to his own tent. At his approach a swarm of mechanics from the factory stood back from the long, low, gray car, the driver who was to relieve him during the night and day ordeal slipped down from the seat and unmasked.

"He's here," announced Dick superfluously. "Rupert—where's Rupert? Don't tell me *he's* gone now! Lestrange—"

But Rupert was already emerging from the tent with Lestrange's gauntlets and cap, his expression a study in the sardonic.

"It hurts me fierce to think how you [151] must have hurried," he observed. "Did you walk both ways, or only all three? I'm no Eve, but I'd give a snake an apple to know where you've been all day."

"Would you?" queried Lestrange provokingly, clasping the goggles before his eyes. "Well, I've spent the last two hours on the Coney Island beach, about three squares from here, watching the kiddies play in the sand. I didn't feel like driving just then. It was mighty soothing, too."

Rupert stared at him, a dry unwilling smile slowly crinkling his dark face.

"Maybe, Darling," he drawled, and turned to make his own preparations.

Fascinated and useless, Dick looked on at the methodical flurry of the next few moments; until Lestrange was in his seat [152] and Rupert swung in beside him. Then a gesture summoned him to the side of the machine.

"I'll run in again before we race, of course," said Lestrange to him, above the deafening noise of the motor. "Be around here; I want to see you."

Rupert leaned out, all good-humor once more as he pointed to the machine.

"Got a healthy talk, what?" he exulted.

The car darted forward.

A long round of applause welcomed Lestrange's swooping advent on the track. Handkerchiefs and scarfs were waved; his name passed from mouth to mouth.

"Popular, ain't he?" chuckled a mechanic next to Dick. "They don't forget that Georgia trick, no, sir."

It was not many times that the cars could circle the track. Quarter of six [153] blew from whistles and klaxons, signal flags sent the cars to their camps for the last time before the race.

"Come here," Lestrange beckoned to Dick, as he brought his machine shuddering to a standstill before the tent. "Here, close—we've got a moment while they fill tanks."

He unhooked his goggles and leaned over as Dick came beside the wheel, the face so revealed bright and quiet in the sunset glow of color.

"One never knows what may happen," he said. "I'd rather tell you now than chance your feeling afterward that I didn't treat you quite squarely in keeping still. I hope you won't take it as my father did; we've been good chums, you and I. I'm your cousin, David Ffrench." [154]

The moment furnished no words. Dick leaned against the car, absolutely limp.

"Of course, I'm not going back to Ffrenchwood. After this race I shall go to the Duplex Company; I used to be with them and they've wanted me back. Your company can get along without me, now all is running well—indeed, Mr. Ffrench has dismissed me." His firm lip bent a little more firmly. "The work I was doing is in your hands and Bailey's; see it through. Unless you too want to break off with me, we'll have more time to talk over this."

"Break off!" Dick straightened his chubby figure. "Break off with you, Les—"

"Go on. My name is Lestrange now and always." [155]

A shriek from the official klaxon summoned the racers, Rupert swung back to his seat. Dick reached up his hand to the other in the first really dignified moment of his life.

"I'm glad you're my kin, Lestrange," he said. "I've liked you anyhow, but I'm glad, just the same. And I don't care what rot they say of you. Take care of yourself."

Lestrange bared his hand to return the clasp, his warm smile flashing to his cousin; then the swirl of preparation swept between them and Dick next saw him as a part of one of the throbbing, flaming row of machines before the judges' stand.

It was not a tranquilizing experience for an amateur to witness the start, when the fourteen powerful cars sprang simul [156] taneously for the first curve, struggling for possession of the narrow track in a wheel to wheel contest where one mistouch meant the wreck of many. After that first view, Dick sat weakly down on an oil barrel and watched the race in a state of fascinated endurance.

The golden and violet sunset melted pearl-like into the black cup of night. The glare of many searchlights made the track a glistening band of white around which circled the cars, themselves gemmed with white and crimson lamps. The cheers of the people as the lead was taken by one favorite or another, the hum of voices, the music and uproar of the machines blended into a web of sound indescribable. The spectacle was at once ultramodern and classic in antiquity of conception. [157]

At eight o'clock Lestrange came flying in, sent off the track to have a lamp relighted.

"Water," he demanded tersely, in the sixty seconds of the stop, and laughed openly at Dick's expression while he took the cup.

"Why didn't you light it out there?" asked the novice, infected by the speed fever around him.

"Forgot our matches," Rupert flung over his shoulder, as they dashed out again.

An oil-smeared mechanic patronizingly explained:

"You can't have cars manicuring all over the track and people tripping over 'em. You get sent off to light up, and if you don't go they fine you laps made."

Machines darted in and out from their [158] camps at intervals, each waking a frenzy of excitement among its men. At ten o'clock the Mercury car came in again, this time limping with a flat tire, to be fallen on by its mechanics.

"We're leading, but we'll lose by this," said Lestrange, slipping out to relax and meditatively contemplating the alternate driver, who was standing across the camp. "Ffrench, at twelve I'll have to come in to rest some, and turn my machine over to the other man. And I won't have him wrecking it for me. I want you, as owner, to give him absolute orders to do no speeding; let him hold a fifty-two mile an hour average until I take the wheel again."

"Me?"

"I can't do it. You, of course."

"You could," Dick answered. "I've [159] been thinking how you and I will run that factory together. It's all stuff about your going away; why should you? You and your father take me as junior partner; you know I'm not big enough for anything else."

"You're man's size," Lestrange assured, a hand on his shoulder. "But—it won't do. I'll not forget the offer, though, never."

"All on!" a dozen voices signaled; men scattered in every direction as Lestrange sprang to his place.

The hours passed on the wheels of excitement and suspense. When Lestrange came in again, only a watch convinced Dick that it was midnight.

"You gave the order?" Lestrange asked.

"Yes." [160]

He descended, taking off his mask and showing a face white with fatigue under the streaks of dust and grime.

"I'll be all right in half an hour," he nodded, in answer to Dick's exclamation. "Send one of the boys for coffee, will you, please? Rupert needs some, too. Here, one of you others, ask one of those idle doctor's apprentices to come over with a fresh bandage; my arm's a trifle untidy."

In fact, his right sleeve was wet and red, where the strain of driving had reopened the injury of the day before. But he would not allow Dick to speak of it.

"I'm going to spend an hour or two resting. Come in, Ffrench, and we'll chat in the intervals, if you like."

"And Rupert? Where's he?" Dick wondered, peering into the dark with a [161] vague impression of lurking dangers on every side.

"He's hurried in out of the night air," reassured familiar accents; a small figure lounged across into the light, making vigorous use of a dripping towel. "Tell Darling I feel faint and I'm going over to that grand-stand café *a la* car to get some pie. I'll be back in time to read over my last lesson from the chauffeurs' correspondence school. Oh, see what's here!"

A telegraph messenger boy had come up to Dick.

"Richard Ffrench?" he verified. "Sign, please."

The message was from New York.

"All coming down," Dick read. "Limousine making delay. Wire me St. Royal of race. Bailey." [162]

Far from pleased, young Ffrench hurriedly wrote the desired answer and gave it to the boy to be sent. But he thrust the yellow envelope into his pocket before turning to the tent where Lestrange was drinking cheap black coffee while an impatient young surgeon hovered near.

The hour's rest was characteristically spent. Washed, bandaged, and refreshed, Lestrange dropped on a cot in the back of the tent and pushed a roll of motor garments beneath his head for a pillow. There he intermittently spoke to his companion of whatever the moment suggested; listening to every sound of the race and interspersing acute comment, starting up whenever the voice of his own machine hinted that the driver was disobeying instructions or the shrill klaxon [163] gave warning of trouble. But through it all Dick gathered much of the family story.

"My mother was a Californian," Lestrange once said, coming back from a tour of inspection. "She was twenty times as much alive as any Ffrench that ever existed, I've been told. I fancy she passed that quality on to me—you know she died when I was born—for I nearly drove the family mad. They expected the worst of me, and I gave the best worst I had. But," he turned to Dick the clear candor of his smile, "it was rather a decent worst, I honestly believe. The most outrageous thing I ever did was to lead a set of seniors in hoisting a cow into the Dean's library, one night, and so get myself expelled from college."

"A cow?" the other echoed. [164]

"A fat cow, and it mooed," he stuffed the pillow into a more comfortable position. "Is that our car running in? No, it's just passing. If Frank doesn't wreck my machine, I'll get this race. And then, the same week, my chum and room-mate ran away with a Doraflora girl of some variety show and married her. I was romantic myself at twenty-one, so I helped him through with it. He was wealthy and she was pretty; it seemed to fit. I believe they've stayed married ever since, by the way. But somehow the reporters got affairs mixed and published me as the bridegroom. Have you got a cigar? I smoke about three times a year, and this is one of them. Yes, there was a fine scene when I went home that night, a Broadway melodrama. I lost my temper easier then; by the time my father [165] and uncle gave me time to speak, I was too angry to defend myself and set them right. I supposed they would learn the truth by the next day, anyhow. And I left home for good in a dinner-coat and raglan, with something under ten dollars in odd change. What's that!"

"That" was the harsh alarm of the official klaxon, coupled with the cry of countless voices. The ambulance gong clanged as Lestrange sprang to his feet and reached the door.

"Which car?" he called.

Rupert answered first:

"Not ours. Number eight's burning up after a smash on the far turn."

"Jack's car," identified Lestrange, and stood for an instant. "Go flag Frank; I'll take the machine again myself. It's one o'clock, and I've got to win this race." [166]

Several men ran across to the track in compliance. Lestrange turned to make ready, but paused beside the awed Dick to look over the infield toward the flaming blotch against the dark sky.

"He was in to change a tire ten minutes ago," observed Rupert, beside them. "'Tell Lestrange I'm doin' time catchin' him,' he yelled to me. Here's hoping his broncho machine pitched him clear from the fireworks."

When the Mercury car swung in, a few moments later, Lestrange lingered for a last word to Dick.

"I'm engaged to Emily," he said gravely. "I don't know what she will hear of me; if anything happens, I've told you the truth. I'm old enough to see it now. And I tried to square things."

[167]

IX

In the delicate, fresh June dawn, the Ffrench limousine crept into the Beach inclosure.

"We're here," said Bailey, to his traveling companions. "You can't park the car front by the fence; Mr. David might see you and kill himself by a misturn. Come up to the grand-stand seats."

Mr. Ffrench got out in silence and assisted Emily to descend; a pale and wide-eyed Emily behind her veil.

"The boys were calling extras," she suggested faintly. "They said three accidents on the track."

Bailey turned to a blue and gold official passing.

"Number seven all right?" he asked. [168]

"On the track, Lestrange driving," was the prompt response. "Leading by thirty-two miles."

A little of Emily's color rushed back. Satisfied, Bailey led the way to the tiers of seats, almost empty at this hour. Pearly, unsubstantial in the young light, lay the huge oval meadow and the track edging it. Of the fourteen cars starting, nine were still circling their course, one temporarily in its camp for supplies.

"I've sent over for Mr. Dick," Bailey informed the other two. "He's been here, and he can tell what's doing. Four cars are out of the race. There's Mr. David, coming!"

A gray machine shot around the west curve, hurtled roaring down the straight stretch past the stand and crossed before them, the mechanician rising in his seat [169] to catch the pendant linen streamers and wipe the dust from the driver's goggles in preparation for the "death turn" ahead. There was a series of rapid explosions as the driver shut off his motor, the machine swerved almost facing the infield fence and slid around the bend with a skidding lurch that threw a cloud of soil high in the air. Emily cried out, Mr. Ffrench half rose in his place.

"What's the matter?" dryly queried Bailey. "He's been doing that all night; and a mighty pretty turn he makes, too. He's been doing it for about five years, in fact, to earn his living, only we didn't see him. Here goes another."

Mr. Ffrench put on his pince-nez, preserving the dignity of outward composure. Emily saw and heard nothing; she was following Lestrange around the [170] far sides of the course, around until again he flashed past her, repeating his former feat with appalling exactitude.

It was hardly more than five minutes before Dick came hurrying toward them; cross, tired, dust-streaked and gasolene-scented.

"I don't see why you wanted to come," he began, before he reached them. "I'm busy enough now. We're leading; if Lestrange holds out we'll win. But he's driving alone; Frank went out an hour ago, on the second relief, when he went through the paddock fence and broke his leg. It didn't hurt the machine a bit, except tires, but it lost us twenty-six laps. And it leaves Lestrange with thirteen steady hours at the wheel. He says he can do it."

"He's fit?" Bailey questioned. [171]

Dick turned a peevish regard upon him.

"I don't know what you call fit. He says he is. His hands are blistered already, his right arm has been bandaged twice where he hurt it pulling me away from the gear-cutter yesterday, and he's had three hours' rest out of the last eleven. See that heap of junk over there; that's where the Alan car burned up last night and sent its driver and mechanician to the hospital. I suppose if Lestrange isn't fit and makes a miscue we'll see something like that happen to him and Rupert."

"No!" Emily cried piteously.

Remorse clutched Dick.

"I forgot you, cousin," he apologized. "Don't go off; Lestrange swears he feels fine and gibes at me for worrying. Don't look like that." [172]

"Richard, you will go down and order our car withdrawn from the race," Mr. Ffrench stated, with his most absolute finality. "This has continued long enough. If we had not been arrested in New York for exceeding the speed limit, I should have been here to end this scene at midnight."

Stunned, his nephew stared at him.

"Withdraw!"

"Precisely. And desire David to come here."

"I won't," said Dick flatly. "If you want to rub it into Lestrange that way, send Bailey. And I say it's a confounded shame."

"Richard!"

His round face ablaze, Dick thrust his hands in his pockets, facing his uncle stubbornly. [173]

"After his splendid fight, to stop him now? Do you know how they take being put out, those fellows? Why, when the Italian car went off the track for good, last night, with its chain tangled up with everything underneath, its driver sat down and cried. And you'd come down on Lestrange when he's winning—I won't do it, I won't! Send Bailey; I can't tell him."

"If you want to discredit the car and its driver, Mr. Ffrench, you can do it without me," slowly added Bailey. "But it won't be any use to send for Mr. David, because he won't come."

The autocrat of his little world looked from one rebel to the other, confronted with the unprecedented.

"If I wish to withdraw him, it is to place him out of danger," he retorted [174] with asperity. "Not because I wish to mortify him, naturally. Is that clear? Does he want to pass the next thirteen hours under this ordeal?"

"I'll tell you what he wants," answered Dick. "He wants to be let alone. It seems to me he's earned that."

Ethan Ffrench opened his lips, and closed them again without speech. It had not been his life's habit to let people alone and the art was acquired with difficulty.

"I admit I do not comprehend the feelings you describe," he conceded, at last. "But there is one person who has the right to decide whether David shall continue this risk of his life. Emily, do you wish the car withdrawn?"

There was a gasp from the other two men. [175]

"I?" the young girl exclaimed, amazed. "I can call him here — safe — "

Her voice died out as Lestrange's car roared past, overtaking two rivals on the turn and sliding between them with an audacity that provoked rounds of applause from the spectators. To call him in from that, to have him safe with her — the mere thought was a delight that caught her breath. Yet, she knew Lestrange.

The three men watched her in keen suspense. The Mercury car had passed twice again before she raised her head, and in that space of a hundred seconds Emily reached the final unselfishness.

"What David wants," she said. "Uncle, what David wants."

"You're a brick!" cried Dick, in a passion of relief. "Emily, you're a brick!" [176]

She looked at him with eyes he never forgot.

"If anything happens to him, I hope I die too," she answered, and drew the silk veil across her face.

"Go back, Mr. Dick, you're no good here," advised Bailey, in the pause. "I guess Miss Emily is right, Mr. Ffrench; we've got nothing to do but look on, for David Ffrench was wiped out to make Darling Lestrange."

Having left the decision to Emily, it was in character that her uncle offered no remonstrance when she disappointed his wish. Nor did he reply to Bailey's reminder of who had sent David Ffrench to the track. But he did adopt the suggestion to look on, and there was sufficient to see. [177]

When Lestrange came into his camp for oil and gasolene, near eight o'clock, Dick seized the brief halt, the first in three hours.

"Emily's up in the stand," he announced. "Send her a word, old man; and don't get reckless in front of her."

"Emily?" echoed Lestrange, too weary for astonishment. "Give me a pencil. No, I can't take off my gauntlet; it's glued fast. I'll manage. Rupert, go take an hour's rest and send me the other mechanician."

"I can't get off my car; it's glued fast," Rupert confided, leaning over the back of the machine to appropriate a sandwich from the basket a man was carrying to the neighboring camp. "Go on with your correspondence, dearest." [178]

So resting the card Dick supplied on the steering-wheel, Lestrange wrote a difficult two lines.

He was out again on the track when Dick brought the message to Emily.

"I just told him you were here, cousin," he whispered at her ear, and dropped the card in her lap.

> "I'll enjoy this more than ever, with you here,"
> she read. "It's the right place for my girl. I'll give
> you the cup for our first dinner table, to-night.

"David."

Emily lifted her face. The tragedy of the scene was gone, Lestrange's eyes laughed at her out of a mist. The sky was blue, the sunshine golden; the merry crowds commencing to pour in woke carnival in her heart. [179]

"He said to tell you the machine was running magnificently," supplemented Dick, "and not to insult his veteran reputation by getting nervous. He's coming by — look."

He was coming by; and, although unable to look toward the grand-stand, he raised his hand in salute as he passed, to the one he knew was watching. Emily flushed rosily, her dark eyes warm and shining.

"I can wait," she sighed gratefully. "Dickie, I can wait until it ends, now."

Dick went back.

The hours passed. One more car went out of the race under the grinding test; there were the usual incidents of blown-out tires and temporary withdrawals for repairs. Twice Mr. Ffrench sent his partner and Emily to the restaurant [180] below, tolerating no protests, but he himself never left his seat. Perfectly composed, his expression perfectly self-contained, he watched his son.

The day grew unbearably hot toward afternoon, a heat rather of July than June. After a visit to his camp Lestrange reappeared without the suffocating mask and cap, driving bareheaded, with only the narrow goggles crossing his face. The change left visible the drawn pallor of exhaustion under stains of dust and oil, his rolled-back sleeves disclosed the crimson bandage on his right arm and the fact that his left wrist was tightly wound with linen where swollen and strained muscles rebelled at the long trial.

"He's been driving for nineteen hours," said Dick, climbing up to his [181] party through the excited crowd. "Two hours more to six o'clock. Listen to the mob when he passes!"

The injunction was unnecessary. As the sun slanted low the enthusiasm grew to fever. This was a crowd of connoisseurs—motorists, chauffeurs, automobile lovers and drivers—they knew what was being done before them. The word passed that Lestrange was in his twentieth hour; people climbed on seats to cheer him as he went by. When one of his tires blew out, in the opening of the twenty-first hour of his driving and the twenty-fourth of the race, the great shout of sympathy and encouragement that went up shook the grand-stand to its cement foundations.

Neither Lestrange nor Rupert left his seat while that tire was changed. [182]

"If we did I ain't sure we'd get back," Rupert explained to Dick, who hovered around them agitatedly. "If I'd thought Darling's mechanician would get in for this, I'd have taken in sewing for a living. How much longer?"

"Half an hour."

"Well, watch us finish."

A renewed burst of applause greeted the Mercury car's return to the track. Men were standing watch in hand to count the last moments, their eyes on the bulletin board where the reeled-off miles were being registered. Two of the other machines were fighting desperately for second place, hopeless of rivaling Lestrange, and after them sped the rest.

"The finish!" some one suddenly called. "The last lap!" [183]

Dick was hanging over the paddock fence when the car shot by amidst braying klaxons, motor horns, cheers, and the clashing music of the band. Frantic, the people hailed Lestrange as the black and white checked flag dropped before him in proclamation of his victory and the ended race.

Rupert raised his arms above his head in the signal of acknowledgment, as they flew across the line and swept on to complete the circle to their camp. Lestrange slackened speed to take the dangerous, deeply furrowed turn for the last time, his car poised for the curving flight under his guidance—then the watching hundreds saw the driver's hands slip from the steering-wheel as he reached for the brake. Straight across the track the machine dashed, instead of following the [184] bend, crashed through the barrier, and rolled over on its side in the green meadow grass.

"The steering-knuckle!" Bailey groaned, as the place burst into uproar around them. "The wheel—I saw it turn uselessly in his hands!"

"They're up!" cried a dozen voices. "No, one's up and one's under." "Who's caught in the wreck—Lestrange or his man?"

But before the people who surged over the track, breaking all restraint, before the electric ambulance, Dick Ffrench reached the marred thing that had been the Mercury car. It was Lestrange who had painfully struggled to one knee beside the machine, fighting hard for breath to speak.

"Take the car off Rupert," he panted, [185] at Dick's cry of relief on seeing him. "I'm all right—take the car off Rupert."

The next instant they were surrounded, overwhelmed with eager aid. The ambulance came up and a surgeon precipitated himself toward Lestrange.

"Stand back," the surgeon commanded generally. "Are you trying to smother him? Stand back."

But it was he who halted before a gesture from Lestrange, who leaned on Dick and a comrade from the camp.

"Go over there, to Rupert."

"You first — "

"No."

There was nothing to do except yield. Shrugging his shoulders, the surgeon paused the necessary moment. A moment only; there was a scattering of the hushed workers, a metallic crash. [186]

From the space the car had covered a small figure uncoiled, lizardlike, and staggered unsteadily erect.

"Where's Darling Lestrange?" was hurled viciously across the silence. "Gee, you're a slow bunch of workers! Where's Lestrange?"

The tumult that broke loose swept all to confusion. And after all it was Lestrange who was put in the surgeon's care, while Rupert rode back to the camp on the driver's seat of the ambulance.

"Tell Emily I'll come over to her as soon as I'm fit to look at," was the message Lestrange gave Dick. "And when you go back to the factory, have your steering-knuckles strengthened."

Dick exceeded his commission by transmitting the speech entire; repeating the [187] first part to Emily with all affectionate solicitude, and flinging the second cuttingly at his uncle and Bailey.

"The doctors say he ought to be in bed, but he won't go," he concluded. "No, you can't see him until they get through patching him up at the hospital tent; they put every one out except Rupert. *He* hasn't a scratch, after having a ninety Mercury on top of him. You're to come over to our camp, Emily, and wait for Lestrange. I suppose everybody had better come."

It was a curious and an elevating thing to see Dickie assume command of his family, but no one demurred. An official, recognizing in him Lestrange's manager, cleared a way for the party through the noisy press of departing peo [188] ple and automobiles. The very track was blocked by a crowd too great for control.

The sunset had long faded, night had settled over the motor-drome and the electric lamps had been lit in the tents, before there came a stir and murmur in the Mercury camp.

"Don't skid, the ground's wet," cautioned a voice outside the door. "Steady!"

Emily started up, Dick sprang to open the canvas, and Lestrange crossed the threshold. Lestrange, colorless, his right arm in a sling, his left wound with linen from wrist to elbow, and bearing a heavy purple bruise above his temple, but with the brightness of victory flashing above all weariness like a dancing flame.

"Sweetheart!" he laughed, as Emily [189] ran to meet him, heedless of all things except that he stood within touch once more. "My dear, I told them not to frighten you. Why, Emily —"

For as he put his one available arm about her, she hid her wet eyes on his shoulder.

"I am so happy," she explained breathlessly. "It is only that."

"You should not have been here at all, my dear. But it is good to see you. Who brought you? Bailey?" catching sight of the man beside Dick. "Good, I wanted some one to help me; Rupert and I have got to find a hotel and we're not very active."

Emily would have slipped away from the clasp, scarlet with returning recollection, but Lestrange detained her to meet his shining eyes. [190]

"The race is over," he reminded, for her ears alone. "I'm going to keep you, if you'll stay."

He turned to take a limping step, offering his hand cordially to the speechless Bailey, and faced for the first time the other man present.

"I think," said Ethan Ffrench, "that there need be no question of hotels. We have not understood each other, but you have the right to Ffrenchwood's hospitality. If you can travel, we will go there."

"No," answered David Ffrench, as quietly. "Never. You owe me nothing, sir. If I have worked in your factory, I took the workman's wages for it; if I have won honors for your car, I also won the prize-money given to the driver. I never meant so to establish any claim upon Ffrenchwood or you. I believe we [191] stand even. Dick has taken my place, happily; Emily and I will go on our own road."

They looked at each other, the likeness between them most apparent, in the similar determination of mood which wiped laughter and warmth from the younger man's face. However coldly phrased and dictatorially spoken, it was an apology which Mr. Ffrench had offered and which had been declined. But—he had watched Lestrange all day; he did not lift the gauntlet.

"You are perfectly free," he conceded, "which gives you the opportunity of being generous."

His son moved, flushing through his pallor.

"I wish you would not put it that way, sir," he objected. [192]

"There is no other way. I have been wrong and I have no control over you; will you come home?"

There was no other argument but that that could have succeeded, and the three who knew Lestrange knew that could not fail.

"You want me because I am a Ffrench," David rebelled in the final protest. "You have a substitute."

"Perhaps I want you otherwise. And we will not speak in passion; there can be no substitute for you."

"Ffrench and Ffrench," murmured Dick coaxingly. "We can run that factory, Lestrange!"

"There's more than steering-knuckles needing your eye on them. And you love the place, Mr. David," said Bailey from his corner. [193]

From one to the other David's glance went, to rest on Emily's delicate, earnest face in its setting of yellow-bronze curls. Full and straight her dark eyes answered his, the convent-bred Emily's answer to his pride and old resentment and new reluctance to yield his liberty.

"After all, you were born a Ffrench," she reminded, her soft accents just audible. "If that is your work?"

Very slowly David turned to his father.

"I never learned to do things by halves," he said. "If you want me, sir—"

And Ethan Ffrench understood, and first offered his hand.

Rupert was discovered asleep in a camp-chair outside the tent, a few minutes later, when Dick went in search of him. [194]

"The limousine's waiting," his awakener informed him. "You don't feel bad, do you?"

The mechanician rose cautiously, wincing.

"Well, if every joint in my chassis wasn't sore, I'd feel better," he admitted grimly. "But I'm still running. What did you kiss me awake for, when I need my sleeps?"

"Did you suppose we could get Lestrange home without you, Jack Rupert?"

"I ain't supposing you could. I'm ready."

The rest of the party were already in the big car, with one exception.

"Take a last look, Rupert," bade David, as he stood in the dark paddock. "We're retired; come help me get used to it." [195]

Rupert passed a glance over the deserted track.

"I guess my sentiment-tank has given out," he sweetly acknowledged. "The Mercury factory sounds pretty good to me, Darling. And I guess we can make a joy ride out of living, on any track, if we enter for it."

"I guess we can," laughed David Ffrench. "Get in opposite Emily. We're going home to try."

THE END